of GILDED FLESH

a novel by

GORDON GRAVLEY

To

Andrea Beatrice Reed,

@lphaEditor.

This one turned out much better

than it was when I started,

thanks to your invaluable Developmental Editing.

Contents

of
GILDED
FLESH

ONE

Of

CRYSTAL EYES AND FATEFUL MEETINGS

"Josef Kronecker," Roth Altbrusser booms at the sight of his first guest. "The clockmaker from Salzburg."

The two of them have never met.

"I can see it in your eyes," Altbrusser says. "I can see the gears behind them working."

He lets go a laugh so big it seems to shake the entire house, from the uppermost social class below to the lowest class above. The clockmaker himself, not often known to smile, can't help but grin at his host's exuberance. With his pink wig and boisterous voice, Roth's presence could fill the grandest of rooms. It is especially refreshing to be greeted at the front door by his host and not a servant.

While they have never met, Josef and Roth are fondly familiar with one another. Josef knows all too well of the Altbrussers' collection, and anyone who appreciates fine timepieces as much as Herr Altbrusser is aware of Josef's work. One of his creations—a mantle clock of porcelain and gilded bronze—sits behind the glass of a Venetian-painted cabinet in the vestibule.

Roth leads him through the apartment where he spies a few of the oddities his evening's hosts are known for: ornamental figurines of hermits and faeries; a three-dimensional diorama of Molière's *Tartuffe*; a seventeenth-century poisons cabinet; a sixteenth-century male chastity belt. Though fascinating, none are what Josef has traveled far to see.

"Helma, my dear," Roth calls out, leading Josef into the interior courtyard. "Helma, did you hear what I said?"

Across the room, Frau Altbrusser turns. She is a presence in her own right, towering over her husband by more than a foot. Add to that the cathedral-like wig she wears and the pair make a startling impression. She turns, and her immense head-dress threatens to topple and take her down to the parquet floor in an avalanche of powder and silk.

"Yes, dearest?"

"I said that I could see the gears turning," Roth

tells her. "Inside the clockmaker's head." With a wink, he laughs again.

Helma lets loose with a vivacious burst of her own as she moves to join her husband and Josef. Her dress's fan-shaped hoop protrudes so widely she must step sideways, with precarious grace, between the display tables about the room.

"It is so lovely you could join us." She offers Josef her hand. He takes it, his fingers dwarfed by hers. "We are such admirers of your work. We couldn't miss this opportunity to meet you."

"I am honored by your invitation," Josef replies. Compliments of his work are not uncommon, yet he finds receiving such accolades uncomfortable.

Herr Altbrusser seizes the moment. "Come, let me show you the latest additions to our collection."

The Altbrussers have no children. Not from lack of trying, but because the rate of child mortality is high these days. As a diversion from this sad reality, Roth and Helma collect, among other things, mechanical figurines that fill the dark corners of their life with gaiety—like the caged bird Roth presents to the clockmaker.

It is small, finch-like. Herr Altbrusser turns a

crank at the back of the pedestal upon which its cage rests, and the little bird comes to life. It flutters its wings and is lifted with the help of a thin, almost imperceptible rod. The bird circles once before landing on a lower perch beside a bowl of seeds. It pecks at the food, gives a cheery chirp, and pecks again. With a shake of its head and a flick of its tail, the finch drops a bit of faux excrement from its tiny anus to the cage's soil-lined base.

Roth lets go a giddy laugh and leans close to Josef. "Like Vaucanson's defecating duck, is it not? Only more delightful, I think. Much more delightful."

Josef nods, his attention upon the hundreds of tiny gears and joints that construct the small bird's anatomy. It is the intricate, complex facsimile of life in which he delights. The little bird chirps again before "flying" back to its upper roost. Josef moves to the next figurine—a cat.

The feline rises from a pillow, arches its back in a stretch, and walks to greet Josef at the edge of the display table. The purr sound emanating from it is impressive. He can't help but give it a stroke, finding its fur realistic to the touch. It takes a drink of milk from a saucer before returning to its nap.

"I wondered if putting the cat beside the bird was a good idea or not." Herr Altbrusser snickers at his own wit.

His wife chortles. "We feared it would eat the poor bird, feathers and all."

Roth gives her a stern glare, indicating that she has dulled his jest. Helma wilts, then slips away to welcome guests that have just arrived.

Josef steps to a life-like, though diminutive, ballerina. He marvels at the details of her complexion, the curve of her neck, the gentle lines of her fingers. With the crank at her pedestal, Herr Altbrusser sets her in motion.

Her movement is as smooth and subtle as a trained dancer. Josef imagines he can see her muscles flex as she pliés, arabesques, and pirouettes before him. Other guests gather and are quieted by her grace. When a gentleman reaches a hand toward her, Josef snatches his arm.

"My apologies," the man says, "but she looks so real. I had to be sure."

"She is very real." Josef releases his iron grasp.

"Just not of flesh." He turns to their host. "Who made her?"

"I'm sorry. I do not know." Roth shrugs. "I acquired all of these pieces from second and third parties. I her found in a warehouse in Berlin draped in linen, poor girl. She deserves the finest silk, don't you think?"

"She's exquisite."

Roth gives him a moment to gaze before taking his shoulder. "Let me show you something truly remarkable."

The proud host takes Josef and his guests to the very thing the clockmaker has braved the Vienna winter to see: a young lad holding a lute—an innocuous yet remarkable object of their own eighteenth-century technology.

On the outside, he is made of wood, painted with a youthful complexion, and dressed in attire common to the Middle Ages. Atop his head rests a cap with a feather. Inside, like the other figurines, he is a complicated mechanism of gears and rods that connect him, through his legs, to the even greater mechanics within the box upon which he sits. It is this machinery that gives the young lad life when the key inserted into his base is wound and activated.

The lad's head tilts back. His mouth opens, and his eyes close, together creating the appearance of laughter. He stands. He is about three feet in height. After giving another laugh, he begins to play the lute. The tone is bright and resonant. As he strums with his right hand, his left moves up and down the frets. His fingers press precisely upon the strings to emit a soothing melody of chords—a song popular during Charlemagne's reign. His body turns from side-to-side, and his head tilts, as though he's as fascinated by those watching as they are of him. The music stops, and the mechanical boy shares one more laugh, winks, then sits back down.

Josef is enraptured. Not by the intricacies of the mechanics or the craftmanship of his appearance, but by the jovial glint in the boy's eyes. He asks about them.

"They are made of the finest crystal," Roth tells him. He then winds the boy up again. The other guests move on, but Josef stays, sitting upon a floral French armchair.

Roth peers at the lad with narrowed eyes. "If only

he could speak."

His wife approaches and clucks her tongue. "Oh, whatever would he say, my dearest?"

"Exactly, Helma. Imagine the things he could tell us."

Josef leans back in the chair. "He's telling us plenty now. A voice would only be distracting."

He gestures for Roth to play the toy again and watches, scrutinizing every detail of the boy's movement—his precision, his human-esque aspect, his joyful presence. Josef is so still studying the toy from his floral chair that guests stop and scrutinize *him*, suspecting he's yet another automaton—though a pensive and brooding one.

"He looks so real," someone observes.

"Yes. But he's so sad," another adds.

"Notice how well the maker has given him the appearance of age. He looks to be fifty or sixty."

"I wonder what he does."

Josef looks up, startling the onlookers. "I make clocks." He smirks. "And I'm forty-five, by the way." They gasp as he stands and walks away to revisit the other displays.

He is least impressed with the caged finch, as there is no true illusion to its flying. He stores that thought in the back of his mind: how to make a bird take flight on its own? He finds humor in the cat. Though it laps milk with a wooden tongue, Josef is reminded of his own cat, Galileo, back in Salzburg. When he reaches to pet it again, a voice comes from behind him.

"Should we be thankful it does not defecate as well?"

It is a woman's voice, with a resonance meant for reading poetry while at the same time commanding an army. That is to say, a voice meant to sweetly charm or deeply cut.

Smiling at the comment, Josef turns to see who spoke.

She is not too delicate, for what army would follow a mere flower? Rather, she stands resplendent as a noble pine, a presence of majestic grace that compels one to kneel. In her eyes, there is knowledge and experience. Josef cannot avert his gaze from the elegance of her round face and her mouth curved like a fine sabre. Before his loss for words becomes awkward, he manages to reply, "It's a sad sign of our times, is it not? This fascination with excrement.”

“An obsession, really.” She extends her hand with an informal, “Klara.”

He takes her hand. “Josef.”

“It is a pleasure to meet you, Josef.”

“Have you seen the young ballerina?”

With the tenderest touch upon her wrist, Josef leads Klara to the ballerina. He asks Herr Altbrusser if he would be kind enough to set her in motion.

Their host beams. “Of course.”

Klara takes in a breath as the girl begins to move. She watches with innocent rapture until the toy dancer unwinds to a gentle stop.

“She’s wonderful,” says Klara. “Please, Herr Altbrusser, play her again.”

Roth obliges with the broadest of grins.

This time, Josef does not watch the clockwork dancer. He sees only Klara.

Her neck. A glimpse of her shoulders. The rising and falling rising and falling bosom. The wrist he’d so boldly touched. And her face. Helen’s face may have launched a thousand ships, but Klara’s could bring them all back. As the ballerina comes to a stop, once more, it is the gleam in Klara's eyes looking directly into his that snaps him from his trance.

"Thank you, Josef, for sharing her with me."

He looks back to the dancer. "A part of me could admire her like this all evening, while another part wishes to tear away her outer layers and examine what's inside."

Klara tilts of her head, bringing a blush to Josef's face.

"I apologize for being crass," he tells her. "I meant her mechanics would be a marvel to expose and study."

"No need to apologize. A bit of crassness is refreshing."

Josef turns and spies the lute player. "May I show you another?"

"Would you, please?"

This time, it is Klara who takes Josef's wrist and allows herself to be led across the room. The clockmaker helps himself to the toy's key and sets the boy to playing. Klara expresses her pleasure with a laugh as bright as a Vivaldi concerto. Her joy is musical to Josef—yet another weapon in her alluring armory.

They play the lad once again, and this time, it is

Klara who watches Josef. She is charmed by the boyish glee on his face, the nimbleness of his hands, and the youthful zeal in his stance. But she does not see him as a boy or by any means elderly. She sees before her a virile man full of life. Fire even. She imagines, for a fleeting moment, straddling him upon a bed of silken sheets and—

A scream echoes through the room.

Everyone turns to a single gentleman, who looks upon the lute-playing boy with an expression of unspeakable horror. His already pale complexion drains to a deathly ashen color. He swoons, then stumbles from the room with another scream. In the wake of his departure, a hush takes over the room. Even the toys seem to wind down in apparent concern.

"All is well everyone." Herr Altbrusser's voice fills the courtyard. "Some people find the wonder of my collection simply too overwhelming. Please, return to your own enjoyment. The figurines are here only for your entertainment. Please, everyone."

Klara leans close to Josef while looking in the direction the panicked gentleman scurried. "That poor man. I've heard of such a thing before. Feelings of the 'uncanny,' I think they call it."

"Yes." Josef nods. "It is not uncommon for someone to panic at the sight of something presumed inanimate suddenly coming to life."

"Presumed? This is just a toy, is it not?"

"Is it just?" He raises an eyebrow.

Klara glows with intrigued delight. "Are you saying this little boy is alive? That he is conscious?"

"What is *consciousness*, exactly?"

"An awareness of self. A cognitive understanding of the world around us. Free will."

Impressed, Josef rethinks his argument. "I wonder, sometimes, just how free our will is. How much of what we think and say is truly our own, or do we merely regurgitate what has come before us?" He pauses to wind and activate the mechanical boy once more. "He plays and stands and laughs and sits just as he always has and always will. It is his purpose. His actions are built into him. What he does is what he is. It's all he knows. Couldn't you say the same about all of us? Don't we all merely tick along——"

"Like toys?" Klara smirks.

"Like automatons, doing only what we've come

to know. Our own actions are nothing but repetitions of what we've done before, are they not? The words we speak have all been said; the stories we tell have all been told. Perhaps we are all nothing more than gears in a great device, sentences in a never-changing tale."

"Yes," Klara contends, "but what does he *think* about what he sees?"

"That is not for me to say," Josef replies. "Perhaps he could tell us."

The two turn toward the lad with the lute. Together, shoulders touching, they watch as the boy grins with that ever-present glint in his eye. Josef and Klara wait with great anticipation for him to share his secret. Then they laugh so heartily that it entices smiles from others in the room.

"It seems he has little to say at the moment," says Klara.

"All the more proof of his consciousness. His vacant response is as authentic and life-like as any human I know. With a touch, he comes alive as much as anyone here."

"Yes, touches will do that, won't they?" The warmth of her tone gives Josef pause. "Sadly, though," she moves even closer to him, "the poor fellow will never have a soul from which he can feel, will he?"

"I'm afraid that would require an alchemist or the conjuring of sorcery, if one believed in such a thing."

"He will never know love or passion."

The heat of her presence leaves Josef without a response; the intimacy of her gaze mutes the entire room. Until a voice familiar to the clockmaker comes between them.

"A discourse on alchemy, Josef?"

He turns to acknowledge the arrival of Dr. Christoph Baeder.

"Or are you weighing man's creativity against God's work again?"

"Can they not be one in the same? Do we not exist but to do God's work?" Josef says. "Or is our existence on Earth meant only to be as purposeful as, say…a shitting duck?"

"Ducks serve a great purpose," the doctor quips. "Their feces fertilize the crops that feed us. And they make a fine Sunday dinner, do they not?"

"We mustn't forget foie gras, either," Klara adds.

"Yes. What would our lives be without foie gras?"

"Klara," says Josef, "please meet Dr. Christoph Baeder. Old friend and fellow conspirator."

Klara takes in the lean gentleman. He wears an understated lavender waistcoat with just a hint of gold embroidery. She appreciates the reserved nature of his modest wig and narrow cane, held lightly but assuredly. He is confident, sans arrogance. A much more respectable figure than most of the physicians she's known. "It's a pleasure to meet you, Herr Doctor," she says. Then, as the doctor takes her hand: "Conspiracy? In what, may I ask?"

"Yes, what schemes have we been stirring of late?" Josef asks his friend.

"Well," Christoph explains, "I'm currently investigating percussive techniques for evaluating conditions within the human body, specifically concerning the heart and lungs."

"Fascinating." Klara is taken more by the doctor's charm than his dry discourse.

Josef scoffs. "Come now. How perfectly mediocre."

"Oh? And what is it you've been toying with?" Christoph asks with raised brows. "Perpetual time, is it?"

"Self-winding mechanics."

With a wink, the doctor tells Klara, "It seems our decadent culture has become so preoccupied with itself that it can no longer be bothered to wind a simple clock."

"Actually," Josef says, "my attention has been upon something of much greater importance than either continuous time or chest echoes."

"Yes?" Christoph and Klara ask in mutual anticipation.

"The extensive benefits of hot chocolate to the mind and the body."

"Hot chocolate?" Christoph says.

"A miraculous beverage, don't you think?"

Klara offers an amused yet disappointed sigh. "The two of you need a lesson in the true meaning of conspiracy, I'm afraid. Will you pardon me? I must speak to our host a moment."

Josef's eyes linger on her as she crosses the courtyard and approaches Herr Altbrusser.

"I suspected I would find you here," Christoph tells him.

"I am predictable that way, aren't I?"

The doctor looks over Josef in a manner only a physician would. With sincere interest, he asks, "How are you doing? How's your heart?"

Josef gives a shrug of strained patience and presents himself as if to say, *How do you think I am?*

"You look flushed. Did you walk here? In the cold?"

"I abhor carriages."

"It must have been a long stroll from Salzburg, then."

"I overcome my blatant aversion when I must."

"Speaking of Salzburg, I'll be visiting next week. I should examine you while I'm there."

Josef acquiesces to his friend's concern. "Of course, Christoph. I'll look forward to your visit. Your company has become far too infrequent. But I'm sure you're not traveling all that way just to see me. What business dealings are you hatching now?"

"Leopold Brunner has requested to meet me. Convenient, as I'm looking to move my practice to Salzburg permanently. Vienna has become far too overrun by doctors. A relationship with Brunner would be all I need to establish myself there."

"Brunner…He's a duke or something, isn't he?"

"Yes, I believe so," Christoph replies with amusement. "I suppose we should acquaint ourselves better with people of our times."

"To what end? He needn't be more than another patient to you. I believe I've made some clocks for him. Several, actually. All I know—or care to know—is that he has fine taste in time-pieces."

Christoph shakes his head. "Are you even aware that France and England are at war again in the Americas?"

"They have forever been at war. How goes it?"

"There's speculation of a coming revolution there."

"I wouldn't be surprised if there were a revolution here soon. In France itself, perhaps." Josef looks over the growing crowd of guests.

"Oh, how I've missed your cynicism, Josef."

The clockmaker brightens as Klara rejoins them.

"I am sorry," she tells the two of them, "but I must be going."

Josef's expression dulls, but he graciously takes her hand and kisses it perhaps a little longer than appropriate, though she doesn't appear to mind.

She smiles. "I feel fortunate to have met you here today, Herr…?"

"Kronecker."

"I can't help feeling it was fate somehow."

"How is it that we could meet again, I wonder? Do you ever visit Salzburg?"

"While I travel extensively, I live there, actually."

Warmth returns to Josef's complexion. "Then I guarantee to find you, Fräulein…?"

She gives a coy tilt of her head. "Perhaps it is I who will find *you*." With a wink, she pivots and leaves the two men where they stand.

Christoph waits only a second before laughing. "Now I see. How silly of me."

"See what?"

"The cause of your flushed appearance."

Josef is quiet as he watches Klara turn and flash him one last, departing smile.

Christoph puts a hand on his friend's shoulder. "She is lovely, isn't she?"

"No," Josef says. "She's exquisite."

TWO

Of

HOT CHOCOLATE

Like most cities of the Holy Roman Empire, at Salzburg's heart sits a castle—Hohensalzburg Fortress. It stands amongst the clouds, looming over the city as the Empire's greatest fortification. Around it lies a patchwork of narrow streets and open squares. From many a window, the castle can be seen, and from many, it cannot, as the front window of Kronecker's Timepieces.

Looking out from Kronecker's, the only view is the goldsmith's shop, not five steps away across a cobblestone lane. Looking in, the view is a bevy of clocks—some made of the finest porcelain or mahogany with bone inlay; some gilded with bronze or brass. Many are small enough for a mantle. A few are as immense as a man. The lull of their ticking fills the space.

Beyond the labyrinth of timepiece displays hangs a dark curtain. Behind that it is the clockmaker's workshop, where the concepts come to life. There's an array of workstations, all strategically positioned for maximum illumination from skylights and windows. For the sunless hours, countless candles line the walls. There are bins of wheels, gears, pendulum rods, and springs, drawers of tools and instruments of precision—all of which have a place in the creation of these complex mechanisms. Shelves of clock-faces await inner workings and sets of hands to bring them purpose.

In a shadowed corner, there is movement: the form of a lean woman bathing with a wet cloth. She touches a hand to the scar on her left temple, acquired from an accident not long ago, and turns to the mirror to examine her crooked eye. Most find her features unremarkable if imbalanced, her head a bit large, her body a bit thin. For that, she is judged as less than attractive—with the exception of her skin, which is as smooth and white as bone china. Her bare skin brightens the darkened corner. Despite her disfigurement, there's a magical glow about her.

She dons the common cloth of a servant—or in this case, a clockmaker's assistant.

Her movement is awkward. Her legs, like her

face, are not what they used to be since the accident. With the help of a cane, she readies the shop for her master's return. There are clocks to wind, floors to sweep, and surfaces to dust. *Dust is a clock's greatest bane,* Kronecker often preaches. The echo of his voice tick-tocks like a pendulum as she goes about her daily tasks.

The sweetest of "meows" comes from the tight corner. Kronecker's assistant smiles and spies the orange head of a cat peeking out from the shadows. "Good morning, Galileo."

"Meow."

"You'll eat soon enough. I expect Herr Kronecker will be arriving from Vienna shortly."

"Meow."

"I would love to someday see Vienna as well. For now, though, I have to get cleaning. Then I have chocolate to prepare."

Hot chocolate: for centuries, a tonic of warriors. The clockmaker did not speak in jest when he claimed it miraculous. Even he cannot manage a day of creative vitality without it. After cleaning the shop, the assistant sets to the elaborate, almost alchemic task of grinding cocoa beans, then combining precise portions of vanilla, milk, cream, and the all-too-critical ingredient of egg yolk over the gentlest of heat. She works with mechanical precision. With a twitch in her right arm—also, acquired from the accident—she creates the impeccably restorative concoction.

The drink is of perfect consistency and temperature when the clockmaker comes in from the biting January winter. Typically, Josef likes to stop upon entering his shop and listen; the rhythmic chatter of the clocks soothes his busy thoughts. But not this morning. Today, he walks in with a burst of energy—a result of the revelation he's carried with him over the many miles from Vienna—and shouts, "Anna!"

Anna emerges from the kitchen with cumbersome steps. She holds a steaming cup in her right hand and her cane in her left.

"Crystal," he says at the sight of her.

"Crystal?"

"For Joop's eyes."

Josef takes the cup from her, briefly holding it to warm his hands before taking a sip. "The finest of crystal, to catch the light and sparkle with life."

"Crystal," she repeats to herself. "To catch light."

Josef heads to the stairs that lead to rooms above the shop.

"How was Vienna?" she asks.

"Exquisite. Inspiring and exquisite." He stops and turns to her before going up. "Oh, I saw Christoph there. He will be coming next week. You'll have his room prepared?"

"Of course. It will be good to see him." She makes a mental note to set up the backgammon, which the two friends love to play. She must also hire someone to ready the doctor's room. She would do it herself if it weren't so difficult—if not impossible—for her to climb the stairs. Anna has always been thankful Herr Kronecker does not adhere to the social protocol of the poorer class living above. God forbid a person of high social standing partake in the common chore of walking up stairs. She rolls her eyes at the thought.

A visit from the doctor will be nice. Except for customers, they rarely get callers. Anna frowns as she remembers something she forgot. Stepping back through the curtain and past the dark corner where she sleeps and dresses, Anna goes to a table where a boy sits. Not a real boy, but a boy not unlike the lute-player at the Altbrussers' apartment. Only this boy is life-size—the size of a small boy—and much more life-like, down to the minutest details of his hair and nails and pores. His "skin" is a thin layer of soft leather, wrapped taut over a skeletal framework of metal and wood. At a glance, in the dim light of the back room, one might think he was real. That is if it weren't for his hollow eye-sockets.

"Good morning, Joop." Anna smiles as she takes his hand.

She wipes his face with a cloth, polishes the alabaster buttons of his shirt, fluffs the lace of his collar, and straightens his slumped posture. As she runs a comb through the threads of silk that are his hair, Anna tells him, "We'll be getting you some eyes soon enough. Don't worry."

⊘ ❧ ⊕ ❧ ⊛

After his first chocolate of the day, Josef is off to his study to work before clients arrive. Although he has a shop full of creations, his most discerning customers prefer to have pieces designed to their specific tastes and unique personalities. There is also clientele with very *particular* needs that appeal to Josef's unparalleled talents in a different way. Take, for instance, the clockmaker's first appointment of the day, Herr Pascal Künzi.

Like many musicians of his era, Pascal was a child prodigy, playing at the age of five and a virtuoso by nine. He'd traveled much of the known world before he was fifteen, but at eighteen, his career came to a horrendous stop. While exiting his carriage in a torrential rain, Herr Künzi slipped to the cobblestone the same instant a thunderclap startled the horses. The harrowing shriek that came from the young pianist as a carriage wheel crushed his left hand will forever be etched in the memories of the bystanders.

Pascal went to a dark place after that. Depression blackened his days; self-destructive yearnings burned through his nights. When he vanished from public view, reclusive beyond reason, many thought him dead.

Such a prodigious gift extinguished too soon, some said.

What a tragedy—such beauty and youth simply gone forever, lamented others.

It was mostly women who mourned for Pascal Künzi, for he is as handsome as he is talented. Although his appearance may be eccentric by conventional standards, it is exactly that peculiarity that is so becoming. Like his hair—black, curled locks that fall loosely to his shoulders. He does not wear the in-fashion wigs because, simply, they itch. Few things are more distracting to a musician than an itch that can't be scratched. Then there is the line of his aquiline nose, the sculpted contours of his lean face, and how his dark, compassionate, deep-set eyes stir even the most jaded of hearts.

To hear himself described in such a way would bring an awkward grin to the young man's face. Though world-wise about many things, he still remains a boy of nineteen, not quite a man. It is his humble nature that most caught the attention of Josef Kronecker, Künzi's greatest admirer.

"Young musicians are as common as syphilis," Josef once said. "But few possess the mature sensitivity Herr Künzi has, his delicate touch upon the keys, or his intuitive interpretation of music."

Having enjoyed Josef's hospitality a number of times prior to the accident, Pascal Künzi is no stranger to the timepiece shop. This particular morning, he enters Kronecker's with agitated anticipation, and the murmur of clocks does little to soothe him. He rushes to hide his leather prosthetic within his cloak as Anna approaches to greet him. She is aware of the loss of his hand, about his emotional turmoil. He really shouldn't find himself in such a flustered state. Yet, he does.

Ever since his accident, the pianist has found empathy toward the downtrodden, the struggling...the broken, and he knows of no one more broken than Anna. Where he once saw only an assistant with bad legs, he now sees a woman who works twice as hard during her daily toil than others. He admires her effort, her fortitude. She is unlike anyone he has ever known. It is this commonality that has fed his adoration for Anna in recent weeks. Having also lost a part of himself, he has come to appreciate all parts of her, damaged or otherwise.

Where most men may notice her silken complexion in passing and move on, Pascal is stirred by how it brings out the natural hue of her lips, along with how the color of her hair changes with the light—one moment as rich as cocoa, the next a warm chestnut. It matters nothing to him that her head is misshapen. He looks into her skewed left eye and sees only a storm he aches to calm.

"How good it is to see you again, Herr Künzi," Anna says. "You're looking well."

The young maestro shakes off his dreamy daze and approaches her with the composure befitting one who has performed in the presence of kings and queens. "Please, Fräulein Klor, call me Pascal."

Anna smiles. "Yes, of course. Then you must call me Anna. Right this way, Pascal."

He watches the laborious meter of her steps. He wishes to help her, to somehow carry her burden. But she doesn't she needs his help. In spite of her injuries, Anna holds her head up with the dignity of royalty and the grace of a saint. He longs to take her thin form and feel the weight of her in his arms, the softness of her ivory flesh against his.

She leads him behind the stairs to the sitting room, with which Pascal is most familiar. He marvels, always, at the walls lined with mahogany bookshelves, over-filled with leather-bound tomes. Above the stone hearth, where a fire burns, hangs the room's only painting: a landscape of an edelweiss-covered hillside.

What *is* new is the Stein fortepiano that sits in

one corner. He looks at it with apprehension. He has not sat at an instrument once during these past months of despondent seclusion. It is too heartbreaking to be only half the musician he once was.

"Herr Kronecker will be with you shortly," Anna tells him. She recognizes, like looking in a mirror, his disengagement. In a tone as warm and comforting as the room, she adds, "Can I bring you something? Tea? Hot chocolate?"

He responds with the sullen shake of his head, his eyes still on the piano.

"How about a shot of rum, then?"

Pascal finally smiles. "No. Thank you, Fräu— Anna. I'm fine." Resisting the urge to watch her leave, he sits.

The pianist waits with his right hand resting upon the wood-and-leather appendage that is now his left, recalling a recent time during which he couldn't bear to look at the hideous object, let alone touch it. The cold, monstrous fingers turned his stomach. But in his current state, he rubs the leathery palm and finds himself strangely soothed.

Josef Kronecker enters. "Dear Pascal. You're

doing well, I hope?"

"Yes, thank you." He stands.

"You're looking fit."

"I've increased my fencing regimen. It's kept me occupied."

"Anna is bringing you something? Hot chocolate?"

"No. She was gracious to ask, as always, but I'm fine"

Josef takes a moment to look at the young man now that pleasantries are out of the way. "No. You're not fine, are you?" He motions for Pascal to approach, then takes his shoulders. "From this day forward, you will be better, my young friend."

Josef looks to a table beside the piano that Pascal had paid little attention prior. Upon it rests a walnut box, the sight of which takes his heart from allegretto to allegro. He attempts to open the box with *both* his hands, fumbling and wrestling with the lid until he steps back, embarrassed by his impetuousness.

"Allow me." Josef gently flips the latch and opens the box.

Pascal gasps, then covers his mouth with his right

hand at the sight of the polished framework, the supple beauty of the steel, and the intricacy of gears and springs and wire. With his fingers, he touches *its* fingers; he caresses its palm. Eyes glistening, the young man grasps the wrist of his new left hand.

"*Magnifique*," he whispers.

"It is, isn't it?" Josef says this with disbelieving modesty that he himself could have created a mechanism of such complexity and engineering: steel rods for bones, wire for tendons, springs for muscles—all replicant of nature's own perfection. "My finest design yet."

"I have no words, Herr Kronecker."

"None are needed. Are you ready to try it?"

Pascal answers by loosening the strap of his current "hand" and letting it drop to the floor with a lifeless clunk. He lifts the new appendage. "It is heavy."

"Yes, as I cautioned. Besides fencing, have you exercised your left arm like Dr. Baeder suggested?"

"Yes." Pascal nods. He inserts the stub of his wrist into the open end of the steel appendage and secures it into place. "It fits…"

"Like a glove?"

They laugh, from relief more than humor. Josef gives Pascal a glove made of the softest leather. "I tried to match the color to your complexion," he explains. "The hand's outer frame has been buffed and polished to be as smooth as glass to aid in the ease of donning and removing the glove."

"It feels so natural." Pascal slips it over his new fingers and up to his forearm.

"I've padded the fingertips so that the steel won't click upon the keys." Josef gestures to the piano. "I ordered this for you. It arrived just the other day."

"A fortepiano. I've considered composing a work for this unique instrument."

The qualms Pascal had about ever playing again wane, overshadowed now by curiosity. He takes his seat on the bench as Josef reaches for a second box, from which he removes a metal disc. Although Josef once explained how the engraved, notched grooves "tell" the hand's fingers what to do, Pascal still marvels at the concentric circles that spiral out from the disc's center. The clockmaker lifts a slit in the hand's glove and inserts the disc into the side of its mechanical wrist.

"Carl Philipp Emanuel Bach's Sonata in B Minor,

the Allegro," Josef tells Pascal. "I apologize that I can fit only a single movement on a disc. You'll have to discreetly exchange them during a performance, but it presents only a minor challenge, I think." With a touch to the back of the prosthetic, Josef activates it. "Just watch first."

Pascal jumps as the hand's fingers begin to move, as agile as his own once were. Then he grins as he recognizes their movement—the notes they are playing.

"It will be a strange sensation at first, and it will take practice to synchronize your hands," Josef says. "I've tried my best to replicate your unique style. Try to imagine—to *feel*—the playing as it were your own, moving with the memory of your muscles."

Pascal watches, mesmerized by the actions of the new fingers with a life of their own, until they suddenly stop. A pang hits Pascal's heart at how still, how lifelessly frozen they become.

"Give it a try." Josef interrupts the solemn moment. "The mechanism winds itself as it plays, so no need to worry about that. Press here to start. There's a pause before it begins, so you can ready your right hand."

Pascal takes a breath and presses the back of the appendage as he was shown. But he waits too long, and the hand begins playing before he's ready.

"As I said, it will take practice." Josef demonstrates how to stop and reset the disc. "You'll also have to learn to use your arm to manage the touch upon the keys."

A part of the young musician wants to run away—again—and vanish in shame. However, the part that desperately yearns to play music wins out, and he tries once more.

And again.

And yet again.

Until…

It is one thing to hear music resonate within a symphony hall. But to experience it emanating from a room in a clockmaker's shop, to feel it fill every corner of an otherwise ordinary space? Anna closes her eyes as she listens.

She moves from behind her curtain and toward the lively, melodious sounds, drawn like Ulysses's men to the Sirens. Lured by the seductive voices of the piano, she finds herself at the door of the sitting room. Each note made under Pascal's skilled fingers dances across Anna's skin, tingles her senses, and penetrates her to a depth rarely ventured during her banal daily routine. She enters the room, cautiously and against her better judgement; she can't seem to help herself.

With awkward but controlled movement, she brings herself to stand just behind Pascal's right shoulder as the sonata ends. The final note sustains and lingers. She rests herself upon it, leans on her cane, and closes her eyes once more. Pascal places his right hand over the now motionless left. With a start, he notices Anna standing behind him.

Josef is, at first, annoyed by her presence; she knows he prefers to meet with clients privately. But instead of chiding her, he tells Pascal, "You must have been aware that Anna would work closely with me. Naturally, she would come to learn of your circumstances. I assure you, there is no better keeper of secrets than she."

Pascal shrinks from her anyway, as though he were naked before her. Although he'd prefer the circumstances were different and that he was naked *with* her, at this moment, he feels vulnerable—more like a boy than a man.

"Pascal, that was…" Unable find the words, Anna instead places a hand upon his shoulder. A tender squeeze from her and his posture straightens. He gives her the slightest of glances and a grateful smile.

"Besides," adds Josef, "this time, she was more than an assistant. She was…an inspiration."

Anna's eyes widen with wary expectation.

"Oh?" Pascal looks between them. "How so?"

Josef gestures to her. "If you wouldn't mind, dear?"

Now it's Anna who is annoyed. She's not sure whether Josef is being petty about her presence in the room or if he is truly sympathetic to their young friend's state. Probably both, she decides, and resigns to her master's request.

With her left hand, Anna reaches for her right and rolls up her frock's sleeve to her elbow. She pinches her skin and tugs at it, hard. Pascal cringes. She yanks at her flesh—or rather, what appears to be her flesh— pulling until it begins to peel from her, as though she were removing…a glove.

Pascal looks to his own new hand and the glove

that covers it, then back to Anna. He takes in a curious gasp at the sight of the steel frame and springs that make up the lower portion of her arm. The mechanics of the appendage are rudimentary compared to his; the steel is rough and dull by comparison, not so polished. The harsh appearance of hers reminds him of an aged woman with swollen joints. Anna demonstrates how, with a twitch of her shoulder, she can make the fingers grasp and release. He reaches his true hand to her true hand with an empathetic touch but she pulls away.

"What happened to yours, Anna?" he asks.

Though his genuine concern touches her deeply, she only offers him a sullen gaze and says, "Another time, perhaps." Anna works to replace her glove while holding her cane. "Be thankful you have the likes of Herr Kronecker in your life." She begins a clumsy exit from the room. "I know I am."

The room settles into silence after her departure.

Josef presents Pascal with a second box and opens it to reveal more discs for the new hand. "I've transcribed the most popular pieces of your extensive repertoire. I'm working on more."

Pascal laughs and asks, "When do you sleep?"

"Sleep is for the dead."

The young man gazes into the empty space where Anna exited the room. Josef presses the box into the pianist's arms, stirring him to respond. "I am thankful for you, Herr Kronecker. Beyond words or financial compensation. I don't know how I'll ever repay you."

"You can invite me to your first—or should I say *next*—performance."

Pascal tucks the box under one arm and grips Josef's hand firmly before taking leave. On his way out, his steps keep time with the ticking of the clocks. He takes a glance around but sees no sign of Anna before departing into the chill.

THREE

Of

SECRECY

At the young pianist's departure, Anna resumes the most relaxing, if not odorous, task of her morning. In the back of the back room, beyond the workstations, behind where Joop the metal boy sits, there is an even more clandestine space. It smells of fur and feces, and it echoes of squeaking, pattering paws, and lots of meowing. Plus a little purring thrown in for good measure.

Galileo, owner of the meows, greets Anna with purrs loud enough to rival a shop full of clocks. He steps into the light from a nearby window, then leaps onto a table because, intuitively, he knows it's difficult for Anna to kneel down to pet him. Anna strokes his arched back. His chirping little meows contrast with his girth.

"Small jumps, Galileo. You know better. To chair, *then* to table."

"Meow, meow—purr," he replies with a head-butt to her hand.

She examines his rear legs. Or rather, what are

now his rear legs.

Strapped to his back end is a pair of spring-loaded hinged rods with padded, paw-like knobs at their ends. The springs compress and release with the movement of his weight. He walks with a slight bounce. By sitting back on the devices, then pushing off with an arch of his spine, he's propelled upward.

When Josef found Galileo some years ago, his legs mangled by who-knows-what-or-how, the pitiful creature simply purred at him. No cries of anguish. No hissing or baring of fangs or even a twitch of his tail. Just a purr to say he had accepted his fate. Josef knew in an instant he'd found a perfect candidate for one of his experiments. Not his first, but what would prove to be one of his more successful.

Anna examines Galileo's hinged hips, knees, and ankles for need of lubrication. The leather strap that keeps the mechanism attached to him has loosened, and she gives it a tightening. All the while, the gentle vibration of the cat's contentment tickles her fingertips.

"Small jumps will keep this from slipping," Anna explains as she has so often in vain.

"Purr, meow."

Sounds echo from beyond the door of the back-back room. "It seems we're late," she tells Galileo. She opens the door to a waft of odors and cacophony of critter chatter.

Before his success with Galileo, the clockmaker had already done numerous experiments. Dr. Baeder was indispensable in trying to keep the animals alive. The ones that survived make up the menagerie Anna now tends. Like the rats, of which there is never a shortage in the city. There's Ramses, with wheels for back legs, and Rupert, whose more technically sophisticated limbs bend and move kinetically in accordance with his movement. Despite the advanced design, Rupert can only lumber along, while Ramses moves quite swiftly thanks to the simplicity of his wheels.

There is also a squirrel Anna named Sneaky, with his flexible, wire-mesh tail, a turtle named Vincent and his four pewter feet, and finally, Annabel, the hopping, wingless raven. Josef has yet to devise a functional replacement for wings. Unaware of the clockmaker's diligent contemplation on her behalf, the sleek, black bird seems happy to live out her life cawing and hopping about.

It's something Anna has often wondered about. She recalls a three-legged dog on her family's farm. It chased chickens, seemingly oblivious to its missing limb. In fact, a prosthetic like Galileo's probably would've just slowed the old mutt down—an opinion she has never shared with Josef. The clockmaker cherishes the cat's back legs, not only for their simple but effective design, but because they were a catalyst for more sophisticated constructs. Like Anna's hand, which culminated into Pascal's. Of all his creations, though, Josef most treasures the eyeless Joop.

A squeak from Ramses's wheels captures Anna's attention. She gives him a piece of dried bread. Annabel caws for one, too. Once done caring for the menagerie, Anna stands before the clockwork boy. From a shelf above his head, she takes a box not unlike the one Pascal left the shop with and opens it. She removes a disc, inserts it into a slot in the boy's back, and moves a lever beside the slot.

Joop straightens his posture with a jolt. His mouth opens grin-like, which brings a smile to Anna. He raises his hands with palms facing her; she does the same, hers facing his. Then she sings:

"Pat-a-cake, pat-a-cake, baker man..."

In rhythm with her voice, they clap their hands together.

"Bake me a cake as fast as you can..."

Alternating right hands to right hands, then left to left.

"Pat it, and roll it, and mark it with a *J*..."

They pantomime the action of patting and rolling dough, mirroring each other's movements. Joop's motion is as fluid and human as hers.

"Put it in the oven for *Joop* today."

When she sings the boy's name, she gives him a poke in his stomach. The mechanical child recoils from her tickle with a voiceless laugh. His hollow eyes close and open. He claps his hands in joy, then leans forward to hug Anna's neck.

As the game is repeated and she sings and claps, Anna's mind wanders to how she came into Josef Kronecker's life—like a broken animal—and her place in it now: his assistant, sometimes his caretaker. *I might as well be married to him, for all I do. All but...*She allows Joop to hug her once more before turning him off. She removes the disc and places it back in its box. *Hell, we even have a child together.*

The bell of the shop's front door chimes. Anna checks the time. She tells Joop, "Pardon me while I entertain His Excellency."

Among the displays, Anna finds Bishop von Bohn perusing and scrutinizing the shop's inventory, just as he's done every morning for months. He never buys, only looks. The sight of his short but sturdy frame wrapped in a black cassock with amaranth trim, hunched forward in studious examination always brings a soothing warmth to Anna. Not because she has an affinity for men of the Church (quite the opposite, actually), but because she likes routine. His presence is a comfort because it is reliable. She imagines these visits serve as a relaxing diversion for him as well. The few minutes spent together each day make for a mutual respite.

"Good morning, Your Excellency," Anna says.

"Good morning, my dear." He points to the black, gold-trimmed mantel clock before him. "This is new, is it not?"

"Yes. Herr Kronecker made that one on a sort of

whim." She moves to stand next to him and leans on her cane. "It just appeared one afternoon, built in the course of a day."

The bishop straightens. "A flash of inspiration?"

"Yes, you might say."

"It is at once so simple yet so elegant. It instills trust and faith."

"Much like yourself, Your Excellency."

The bishop gives her a grateful nod. He tours the other displays with casual interest before returning to the black mantel clock.

"Might you like to take this piece home with you today?" Anna asks.

"No, thank you. Perhaps another day."

"I can hold it for you, if you like. Indefinitely, until that day."

"You are very kind, but that won't be necessary." The bishop raises his head and closes his eyes to the drone of the clocks, as though enjoying the gentle notes of a symphony. He adds, "However, feel free to dissuade others from purchasing it, if you're so inclined."

"Of course. Be well, Your Excellency."

Dr. Christoph Baeder enters Kronecker's Timepieces early one morning a few days later. Anna has a cup of strong black tea waiting for him, for the doctor does not care for chocolate. They greet each other cordially, if not a bit formally. Later, when she serves the mid-day meal, he will invite her to join him and Josef. She always looks forward to an afternoon of food and conversation with the two most important people in her life.

Josef and Christoph met at the Faculty of Medicine of the University of Vienna. Josef attended only a year, as he found the anatomy of clocks more to his liking than that of his fellow humans. He also preferred their company, with the notable exception of Christoph Baeder. They struck a rapport that has lasted decades—a friendship for which Anna is forever grateful. It saved her life. When she was tossed down a rocky ravine to die, it was the exceptional skills of the doctor and clockmaker that mended her.

Dr. Baeder shows himself to his room, up the stairs and adjacent to Josef's. He then seeks out his friend, finding him in his studio with an array of drawings and schematics on a table before him.

Unsurprisingly, the clockmaker is unaware of Christoph's presence. He marvels at the intense focus of Josef before speaking.

"What now?" he says. "Are you looking to replicate the human brain? Or perhaps a mechanized soul?"

Josef's stupor lingers a moment until he manages to drag his gaze away from the schematics. "Christoph. You're early. I would have welcomed you at the door had I known."

"No, you wouldn't have." Christoph looks at the pile of drawings. "No matter. I'd much rather be greeted by Anna than a cantankerous old man on his best day."

Josef laughs. He rounds the table, and they embrace. "Oh, Christoph, you should have seen it. Pascal's hand worked to perfection. He took to it almost immediately."

"I'm sorry to have missed it."

"I expect it won't be long before he plays for an audience again. He's truly a remarkable young man."

The doctor grins at his friend's youthful enthusiasm. "You'll be sure to let me know when he does."

"Of course, of course. But he doesn't know of your involvement, remember, or that you know of his circumstances. He's very sensitive about it."

"Only Anna and I know?"

"Yes. Well, outside the carriage driver, those who heard his screams, and the surgeon who removed his hand."

"And his family," Christoph adds.

"He has none that I know of. He's been very much alone through all of this."

Silence falls between them. Josef sighs. "I can't help but wonder about the futility of secrets."

Christoph only smiles.

"Yes, I know we all have our secrets."

"They're what make us interesting, don't you think?"

Josef shrugs. "Yet they can lead to great unpleasantness when eventually brought to light."

"As I said: *interesting*."

"They always come to light, is my point. Just another of life's inevitable unpleasantries."

They fall silent again until Christoph says, "I would like to examine you sometime today."

"Speaking of unpleasantries," Josef replies. "If you must. But I refuse to be prodded until I've had something to eat."

◎ ❧ ◉ ❧ ◎

Anna lays out a tripe soup with juniper berries, and pigeon roasted with wine and chestnuts for Josef and Christoph. By the look on Christoph's face, he is quite pleased. Anna is invited to join them; however, it is Josef who requests her company rather than Dr. Baeder. Her sedate acceptance hides her elation for one of her fondest pleasures: dinner with the doctor and the clockmaker. She settles herself into a chair to Christoph's left and across from Josef.

"How have you been doing?" Christoph asks her.

"As well as could ever be expected, thank you."

"I should examine you as well while I'm here. If you don't mind."

"Of course."

As they dine, the gentlemen begin a dialog on war, particularly the one progressing into southern India. Anna allows them to continue through the soup, but before the pigeon, she finds she must interrupt. "War is as ubiquitous as boiled beef. Perhaps we could find a more interesting topic."

Christoph offers news of an academy being established in Vienna. "It will be for the education of scholars," he explains, "to accommodate our growing relationship with the Ottoman Empire and its various cultures."

Josef shares talk of a tunnel through Mönchsberg Mountain being planned. But the cream of the conversation comes with dessert, which today is a three-peaked souffle and a raspberry sauce that's been preserved since autumn. Christoph, always the gentleman, saves Anna the trouble of standing by serving the dish himself. Once they have enjoyed the first taste of Nockerln, the doctor brings up the subject of secrecy. Anna puts down her spoon and listens with a patient ear.

"I contend," Christoph says to her, "that our secrets make us who we are and are what make us intriguing to others."

"Only if others suspect we *have* secrets," Anna replies.

"We all have secrets," says Josef.

Christoph nods. "It's human nature to be suspicious of others. If our secrets are who we are, then that is what draws us to one another. It doesn't matter if we don't know what those secrets are; the allure is still there. Greater, I think, if we *don't* know. In fact, the deeper—"

"And darker?" Anna offers.

He nods again. "It creates…an air of mystery. Ever wonder why you find a certain person more attractive than another? I think it's because of what we don't know about them."

Anna considers the postulation. With a tilt of her head and a shrug of her shoulders, she accepts the doctor's theory, then takes a bite of souffle.

"Josef, however, has the idea that we should have no secrets, that our souls should be bare for all to see— thus, avoiding the discomfort and unpleasantness of their discovery."

"What's wrong with unpleasantness?" Anna asks. "I find there's something attractive about discomfort, something sensual about melancholy."

"Truths always come to light," Josef says. "One way or another. Perhaps the sooner they are exposed, the better. Then everyone can get on with their lives."

"You think they would 'get on' just as before? The unveiling of truth changes people, don't you think? And not necessarily for the better." Anna pauses to find the right words. "The sharing of secrets should be left to only the closest of friends…and lovers."

Anna finds her gaze lingering on Josef and turns away. She wonders if he has any clue about *her* secret: her feelings for him. If their eyes were to meet at that very moment, would he see it? What would he feel about such a truth? She fears what his reaction would be—no matter *what* it would be.

"What of family?" Christoph asks.

"No," she answers, perhaps a bit sharply.

Josef and Christoph look to each other. Deciding not ask Anna to elaborate, Josef offers what he thinks will lighten the moment: "Where does our young pianist fall, with *his* secrets?"

Anna doesn't respond. Pascal's affections for her are really no secret. She waits to see where Josef is taking the conversation.

He tells Christoph, "Young Pascal exhibited some reluctance toward his new hand, embarrassed about his apparent inadequacy. Anna, invaluable as always, eased his ill feelings by showing him he is not alone. She helped him realize the possibilities."

Christoph extends a sympathetic touch to Anna's arm. "You showed him your hand?"

"Not by my choosing. But, yes," she says, her voice cooler than before.

"But it proves my point," Josef says. "The freeing of secrets. The positive end to truths shared."

Anna turns a gentle smile on the doctor, and then a not-so-gentle scowl on the clockmaker. "As I said, it was not by my choosing."

Josef waves a hand. "Does that matter? Aren't you relieved, even a little, from the burden of shame?"

"I am not ashamed. I'm…" She looks down at what has been her right hand for over a year now. With a twitch, she opens it. Then closes it. Not exactly humanlike, but functional. She considers Pascal's device, a marvel of engineering that will give beauty to the world.

"You say we should have no secrets," Anna finally continues, "yet you create veils—blindfolds even. If, as you say, the painful discovery of truth is inevitable, what will become of Herr Künzi when his charade is revealed? The public may be amazed at what *you've* done, but what will they think of *him?*"

Christoph leans forward with a growing grin, piqued by her argument.

"I wonder," she says, "how the world would embrace a one-handed pianist? With compassion and acceptance? How wonderful it could be for him to compose the first concerto for right hand only…Or to become a conductor of his own great symphonies. Isn't it better, as you propose, the truth be known now rather than after an elaborate deception?"

Christoph's grin becomes a smile as wide as his slim face will accommodate.

Anna goes on. "I often question whether or not I could do with only one hand. Clean, cook, prepare hot chocolate. I imagine it's possible. People have done more with less. I've seen a street vendor with no arms. The courage that must take…Not like going-to-war courage, but the strength to face each and every day." She looks again at her right hand and the veil of its flesh-colored glove. "I wish for Pascal to have that courage one day, before the painful truth rears itself." She looks down at her souffle. "If you'll excuse me," she says.

Christoph and Josef both assist her as she awkwardly rises, then watch as she leaves, accompanied by the dull tapping of her cane.

Josef sits solemnly. "It seems I am now a hypocrite."

Christoph laughs. "There have been much worse things said about you."

While Christoph examines Josef, Anna tends to the clocks—a mundane chore she finds soothing; the lull of the ticking lends itself to meditative contemplations. Thoughts of things great and small. Of life. Of men.

Anna has always been aware of Pascal's romantic feelings for her. What woman would not enjoy the attention of an elegant young man? One who is not vulgar with immaturity, that is. She remembers the first time she saw him perform, his zealous fingers upon the keys. Her body warmed as she imagined being played by such youthful, sensitive hands—or *hand*.

While he's nineteen and there are only six years between them, the difference somehow makes her feel worn. How can he not see how damaged she is? What could she ever have to offer him—or any man?

Stop it, she scolds herself. *Self-pity has no place here.*

Anna shakes off the creeping malaise of discouragement that plagues her waking hours. Literally shakes. In doing so, her right hand pops open. She laughs like she's been surprised by a magician's trick.

The device makes her think of Christoph and Josef, both of whom are older than her. She has never considered Christoph as anything more than a caring older brother. Surely, he is handsome, even flawless in many ways. He is kind. Empathetic. Yet…clinical. His manners and appearance exhibit the scientific, sterile nature of his profession. One might think that description equally befits the clockmaker, who's a fabricator of cold, functional perfection. But it is from a source of great fire that Josef forges his creations; it's that spark that lights his eyes and stokes his very being.

The clockmaker's appearance is often rough. When working, he can't be bothered by matters as trivial as hygiene. He never wears a wig. He'll go days without shaving. To her unspoken delight, Anna has had to give him a sponge bath on occasion while he stood at his drawing table because he refused to stop working. The water glistening over his lean contours had aroused her to the core.

She also knows no other man who would have risked their own safety for her. It was Josef who traversed the rocky ravine where she had been thrown and left to die after being beaten and crippled by an aristocrat whose advances she refused.

That night was a clear one. The moon was full, and the stars of fate aligned for a brief moment as Anna lay there. Josef was on one of his midnight walks when, for the flicker of a second, he glimpsed the glow of flesh in the moonlight. He saw her arm reaching upward to the sky. If not for her bare skin, he would have thought her nothing more than a pile of discarded garments and kept walking.

Instead, he ventured down the precarious slope, stumbling until he came to the shocking sight of a woman twisted amongst the rocks, crumpled like unwanted debris. She was as cold as the stones around her, but she breathed. He hurried to find a pair of men who could help lift her to the road and carry her to

Landeskrankenhaus, the general hospital of Salzburg. His friend Dr. Baeder happened to be there on one of his visits from Vienna. Again, an alignment of the stars.

"She should be dead," had been Christoph's initial prognosis. He intended only to make her comfortable in her final hours.

But she did not die.

"She seems to possess an unearthly power to live," Christoph told Josef.

Because she'd been left in the care of one of the best men medical science has to offer, and because she would not willingly leave this earthly plane, Anna now cleans clocks and sets time. She contemplates men and life and what might be. To hell with self-pity.

"Pardon me," comes a voice of fine, tempered steel. "I'm looking for Herr Kronecker."

Anna turns, and there stands perhaps the most exquisite-looking woman she has ever seen.

FOUR

Of

BITTER GRACE

Josef sits upright on the edge of the sofa and places his left hand upon the oaken armrest. On his face, he wears a look of resigned tolerance as his friend, who has slipped into the role of physician, gives him a thorough examination.

He first checks Josef's pulse for pace and quality of pressure. After a minute, he nods in satisfaction and proceeds to examine Josef's body with his eyes and his nose. He nods again, neither seeing nor smelling anything unusual. Then he has Josef lie down. After palpating his head, chest, and abdomen, Christoph allows him to sit back up. "Any chills or out-of-the-ordinary physical symptoms?"

"Nothing beyond the coldness of your hands."

Christoph ignores the commentary he has come to expect from his most acerbic of patients and begins the percussive part of the exam, sharply tapping and listening to areas of Josef's chest.

"I'm sorry I am without urine for you to taste." Josef smirks.

"Techniques to test sugar levels chemically are being developed, I'll have you know."

Josef feigns a look of interest.

"There have been great advancements in medicine of late. Enough to keep you alive longer than you probably deserve."

Josef laughs. "I'm glad someone agrees with me that there are always advancements to be made, better ways to do what has always been done."

Christoph steps back and gives his friend another look from head-to-toe. "Josef, you are as fit as a much younger man. In most respects, anyway."

"Walking is what does it. I keep trying to tell you. Walking."

"At all hours still? Day or night?"

"Especially night. Fewer distractions, and the air is most invigorating."

"Fewer people to notice if you should drop dead." Christoph gives him a look of disapproval.

"I'll be dead. What will the time of day matter?"

"It wouldn't kill you to take a carriage once in a while."

"It might."

Christoph stops with a rueful sigh. "I'm sorry, Josef. You know I didn't mean to——"

Josef raises a hand. "I understand. No need to apologize."

"But don't you think it's time you overcame your fear of carriages?"

"I don't fear them, Christoph. I loathe them. I despise them. If there were a single word to describe the single greatest hatred for something, I would use it for carriages."

"It's been years since the accident."

"Yes. As many years as a young boy's life."

Christoph shakes his head at the futility of arguing. "I'd like to listen to your heart once again before I conclude." He leans in and puts an ear to Josef's chest. "Like a clock. But it could be better."

"Of course."

"There's a sound—Mmur—Mmur…"

"M-mur?"

"That's how I would describe it. A *murmur*, you might say. It concerns me."

"It just so happens—"

Anna enters the room. She catches a glimpse of Josef's taut physique as he closes his shirt—nothing she hasn't seen before, yet she finds herself taking pause.

"Yes? What is it?" Josef asks.

"There's a lady here to see you, without an appointment. She says she knows you."

The two men look at each other with intrigued grins. Anna can't help noticing how Josef's eyes brighten. A mere moment later, he is fully dressed and, followed closely by Christoph, seeks out the woman, who is busy perusing his shop.

"Klara. What a delightful surprise." Josef takes her hand.

Her charmed smile grows at the sight of Christoph. "Dr. Baeder? Lovely to see you as well."

Christoph takes her hand next. "Your timing couldn't have been better," he tells her.

"What brings you here? Can I offer you something?" Josef looks for Anna, who is nowhere to be found. "We have just recently dined, I'm afraid. A bit of

Nockerln, perhaps?" He looks again but does not notice his assistant, who lingers around a nearby corner.

"No, thank you. I'm fine," Klara says.

"What brings you here?"

"Well, after we met, I came to learn that I had been in the presence of the renowned Josef Kronecker, maker of exceptional timepieces. I couldn't resist imposing upon him for a personal tour of his shop."

"It's no imposition at all. You came all the way from Vienna to look at clocks?"

"You traveled *to* Vienna to look at toys, did you not?"

"Well, that was for…research."

"Perhaps I could say the same." She smiles. "Besides, you may recall I live here in Salzburg."

"Yes, I remember now. I apologize. I find that, in your presence, my memory loses a bit of its efficacy."

"These aren't just any clocks, are they?" She looks about. "Something tells me each has a story to tell."

"Oh, this place is full of stories," Christoph says.

"I'd love to hear a few of them, if you wouldn't mind."

"I can't think of anything I would enjoy more,"

Josef tells her, lost in the eyes of a woman few men, if any, have likely ever said 'no' to. "I have some time before my next client arrives."

"Client?"

"A special request. It seems all I do lately. Another work with another story."

"I'm intrigued." Klara takes a step closer.

Josef inclines his head. "Another time."

"I'm afraid I must take leave," Christoph says. "Besides, I've already heard all his stories and know how they end." With a kiss to Klara's hand, he flashes a wink at Josef and adds, "All but one, that is."

"I didn't mean to chase you off, Dr. Baeder," Klara says.

"You've done nothing of the kind. Really, I must be going. Until next time."

As Christoph leaves, Josef tries to compose himself. Klara points to a mantle clock with a dark walnut base, graceful gold hands upon a pearl face, and classic Roman numbers of black onyx. "Let's begin with this one. So striking. I've never seen another like it."

"I would certainly hope not."

She gives him a curious look.

"I made several, actually, of the same design, for a particular marquis. It's not an unusual request, the intention being to share something unique among family or dear friends. This gentleman, however, wanted one made for each of his many lovers."

Klara raises an eyebrow.

"Yes, he was not the shrewdest of gentlemen. While one of his lover's was attending an event at the home of another, she spied the very same clock upon the mantle. The veil of deceit unraveled rather quickly, as you can imagine, and came to a raucous climax when the marquis's wife became enlightened to the affairs."

"How many clocks did you make, if I may ask?"

"Nine."

"Oh, my."

"The affairs themselves were of little concern to the marchioness. What truly upset her was that she had not received a clock of her own."

Klara's laugh fills the shop. "How is it you still have this one?"

"I made it for the marchioness. Just in case."

Klara saunters to another time piece. It is the most unusual in the shop, partly due to its size and partly due to its appearance.

The clock's face is three feet in diameter, set within an oaken frame. Inlaid marble numbers decorate its copper surface. Ornate iron hands are installed over the face and possess a royal sort of presence. What's most unusual is that there is no cabinet; the inner workings are exposed to see and touch, if one so desired.

"What was the inspiration behind this one?" Klara asks.

"It's an experiment in perpetual mechanics."

"Perpetual?"

"Everlasting. It never needs to be rewound."

Klara peers at the intricacies of the clock's system: a series of interconnected pendulums and ball-bearing wheels that keep themselves in constant motion with the aid of a tightly coiled, self-winding spring.

"It's based on a number of different devices," Josef explains, "all experiments in perpetual motion themselves. Like da Vinci's overbalanced wheel, there at its core. In theory, it should eventually run out of self-sustaining energy and stop. That's where the self-winding coil comes into play. It creates its own energy, you might say, to keep it going."

"How long has it been running?"

"A couple of years now, with no sign of slowing."

"It's magnificent, Josef. It belongs on a tower overlooking the square for everyone to see."

He shakes his head. "It would be wasted on those who would merely look to know how much time before their next self-serving indulgence."

Klara smiles. "In most men, cynicism is disappointing. But in you, it's…charming."

Hiding his blush, the clockmaker turns to continue the tour. Thirty minutes and as many stories later, Count Wilhelm Meusberger strolls into the shop.

There are any number of reasons why someone would question Count Meusberger's ability to dance. To begin with, he is as round as he is tall; his shape and stature do not inspire images of agility and finesse. His breathing is so labored upon entering a room that the idea he'd possess the stamina required to move rhythmically for longer than a second is questionable, if not unbelievable. A person is more inclined to lend him a hand to sit rather than join him in a minuet. Yet, the count loves to dance.

No, the count *loves* to dance.

Count Meusberger is nimble as a sprite with his footwork, graceful as a swan in his turns and bows, and as confident as a conductor with his arms and hands. His reputation upon the ballroom floor is known throughout the Holy Roman Empire. What most people don't know is that the count is nearly crippled. The normal function of his stout, strong legs has been compromised by ulcers on his feet. It is this unfortunate physical circumstance that brings him to the clockmaker's shop this day and interrupts Josef's interlude with Klara.

"Count Meusberger," she says upon seeing him, "how well you are looking."

"And you, my dear," replies the count with a belabored breath.

"You know the count?" Josef asks.

Klara smirks. "I know many people, Josef."

"The Count is the client I've been expecting, so—"

"So, I shall wait."

"If you're so inclined. This shouldn't take long. I'd love to show you more."

Klara gives him a glance that makes him resent

his scheduled appointment. "That would be delightful."

Josef's resentment passes quickly; Count Meusberger is not one you can easily stay mad at. His zest for life thaws any indignation, and just the sight of his exuberance brings a genuine light to the clockmaker's face. In the privacy of the sitting room, Meusberger begins: "Herr Kronecker, you look so very well. You must be spending time in the company of an exceptional woman."

"Perhaps," Josef replies, wanting to offer no more than that. "How can I serve you today, sir? How are your legs?"

The count struts about the room, humorously feigning an air of hauteur. With the almost imperceptible motion of his mid-section, he propels himself forward until he circles to a stop and presents himself to Josef. Then, he lets down his pantaloons. They drop to the floor, revealing a structure of steel and brass around his swollen, afflicted legs. The framework supports his weight like his own bones no longer can and moves him with the help of an intricate puzzle of springs and hinges in ways his muscles no longer do. Or ever did, in fact.

It is the subtle movement of his hips that allows the legs to "walk" and to move the count forward. A complex pendulum system within each appendage perpetuates the motion, giving the impression of strolling along—for three or four steps at a time, at least. It is by the count's rhythmic motion and innate poise that he is able to advance himself forward with onlookers none-the-wiser to his condition.

Pleased, Josef kneels down to examine his creation. He grasps the steel in various places, checking the structural integrity, and touches the springs to confirm tautness. He inspects the hinges.

"You're keeping these routinely lubricated?" he asks.

"Yes, like *clockwork*." The count chortles.

Josef grimaces. He's heard one too many clock jokes. Satisfied, he stands. "The springs exhibit a bit of wear. Otherwise, everything looks in order. You've had no difficulties with them?"

"None. They work better, I think, than my own legs ever did."

"What, then, is the reason for your visit, Count Meusberger?"

"My allemande is not what I would like it to be."

"I see."

"That particular dance is the closest I can get to a woman without suffering the repercussions of vulgarity," the count jests.

The humor is wasted on Josef as he falls into contemplation. There are challenges in the allemande to be considered: balancing upon one foot; graceful, hopping steps while turning, arms interlaced with one's partner—all done to a lively two-four time.

"It most likely has to do with the worn springs," Josef says. "Have you been cognizant of your weight, Count Meusberger?"

The count looks away shyly.

"I can make changes to enhance your performance of the allemande, but it will be equally improved by your reduced intake of Linzer torte."

Recoiling springs, Josef thinks, are the key. Springs as elastic as tendons, but of less bulk. Perhaps an adaptation of da Vinci's designs? Or maybe a type that has yet to be invented. These are the challenges upon which the clockmaker thrives.

It isn't long before Klara has seen every clock in the shop. Soon her attention is drawn to a particular curtain and what lies behind it.

There she finds the workroom. She spies Anna, who does not notice her, and Klara watches her go through bins of gears. She makes the assistant out to be in her mid-twenties. A bit thin and potentially pretty, if not for her disfigurements. Klara envies her complexion and is especially intrigued by how Anna's right hand grasps so stiffly. And what of the odd twitch in her shoulder? Klara leans in to observe.

Anna looks up.

"I'm so sorry," Klara says. "I did not mean to startle you."

"Is there something I can help you with?" Anna's tone is sharp and her voice wavers as she regains composure. "Herr Kronecker is not back here, if you need to speak with him further."

"No. He asked me to wait." Only a slight look of embarrassment befalls Klara's face. "Please, excuse my impropriety. My curiosity compels me to wonder what lies behind closed doors or drawn curtains. I could not resist."

"You're welcome to wait." Anna gestures back toward the black curtain and the shop beyond.

Klara does not move. Instead, she looks about the area with interest until her gaze stops on Anna's clothes: a bodice, held together with simple clasps, wrapped around an unusual dress that appears more like a cloak. Klara does not know that Anna's garments have been designed around her physical limitations; she only sees it as unconventional. She notes Anna's cane.

"Are you not well, my dear?" Klara asks. "Perhaps you should lie down?"

"I was in an accident a short time back. This is now my permanent state, I'm afraid. I manage well enough."

"How does a woman such as yourself become a clockmaker's assistant? It seems…"

"Inappropriate?"

"Unlikely."

Anna gives the question consideration. "You might say I was *thrown* into it."

"I did not get your name."

"Annamarie."

"Annamarie…?"

"Klor."

"Annamarie Klor," Klara repeats, with emphasis on the last name. "I am Klara. Are you aware our names come from a similar origin?"

Anna shrugs.

"Klara and Klor. They come from a word that means *pure* and *beautiful*. Quite fitting in our cases, don't you think?"

"Oh, I did not know that." Anna turns shy. She cannot recall the last time anyone called her beautiful. In fact, has anyone *ever* called her that? Perhaps the farm boy of her youth…He had professed his love, but had he ever told her she was lovely or enchanting? She cannot recall. But she can remember his eyes. He didn't need to say anything: it was all in the way he looked at her. It was all in those eyes. Anna becomes aware of Klara's voice once again, drawing her back to the present, and responds with a vacant, "Yes? I'm sorry. You were saying?"

"Your first name—Annamarie—means *bitter grace*, I believe."

Bitter, most certainly, Anna thinks. *But grace?*

"Most call me Anna, madam."

"What is it you do as an assistant, Anna?"

Anna collects herself and explains, "I prepare meals, and I clean—dirt is the bane of clocks. I collect parts and organize them into bins for individual projects, like I was doing here. You could say I minimize the tedium."

Having already wandered the room with her eyes, Klara now does so with her feet. She stops at the door that hides the menagerie and wrinkles her nose.

"What is that odor?"

Anna moves to put herself between Klara and the door. "I'm not sure—"

"It smells like rats." Klara reaches for the door.

"No!" Anna grabs Klara's arm with her left hand.

Klara pulls back, at first affronted by the assistant's brashness, she then realizes her own bold behavior. She nods and smiles an apology, then spies a bed in the corner. Beside it, there is a modest armoire and an equally plain dressing table.

"What is this?" Klara's face is overtaken a repulsed sneer. "Where vagrant guests sleep?"

"No. This is where I sleep."

Klara's eyes widen.

"I can't climb stairs. Otherwise, I'd take a room above the shop. This space offers me sufficient comfort and privacy."

"My dear, you've been sequestered to a dark corner loose with rats."

"We don't have *loose* rats," Anna tells her. "Perhaps you should wait for Josef—er—Herr Kronecker out front now."

"No. But perhaps I should *have a word* with Herr Kronecker."

⊙ ❧ ⊙ ❧ ⊙

Pantaloons on the floor, Count Meusberger stands before the clockmaker. "Well, Josef, will I be able to dance as I wish?"

Josef looks from the count to his table of sketches and calculations, then back to the count, again and again, in silence. Silence that is pierced by the opening and closing of doors and the stomping of feet from other parts of the shop. Josef examines his notes; he mulls his calculations. He refrains from giving an answer as the noises loom closer and gestures for Meusberger to cover himself up.

A moment later, Klara throws open the door to Josef's study. She gets a full view of the framework wrapping the count's legs just as he conceals himself. However, that is not her present concern.

"Herr Kronecker, I'd like to have a word with you."

"Klara?"

"Tell me how it is you find this woman's living conditions acceptable?"

Anna appears in the doorway behind Klara, timid but with great curiosity. Josef has no time to respond before Klara continues.

"You allow her to sleep and dress in a corner rampant with rats?"

Josef looks helplessly to Anna, who looks away. "I assure you, Klara," he finally says, "we are not rampant with rats."

"Perhaps not to the eye, but the odor says otherwise. It's a smell I'm more than familiar with, and its consequences are far too dire to be ignored, don't you think?"

Count Meusberger, having taken refuge behind a

changing screen, offers, "An incident of the plague occurred recently in Constantinople."

His input goes unacknowledged as Josef attempts to explain. "I—Anna has never objected to her accommodations before. I never—"

"Of course not," Klara replies. "I gather she is somehow indebted to you and doesn't feel it is her place, so I am objecting for her. Is she a mere servant? Or is she an assistant—a partner—with you in your work?"

"Well…"

"There must be some other space available where she could enjoy a little comfort." Klara takes in a deep, calming breath. "And dignity."

"At this time," says Josef, "she cannot climb stairs."

"There are plenty of rooms down here. Perhaps this one. Or the drawing room. Or the one with the piano."

Anna smiles at the thought of that.

Heavy silence fills the space as Josef contemplates the idea. He knows it is in *his own* best interest to at least resign to, if not accept, the proposal. "Very well." He looks past Klara to Anna. The delight in her eyes reminds him that, of course, it is actually in *her* best interest. "Anna," he tells her, "my deepest apologies. I will arrange to have your things and a proper bed moved into the room of your choosing at the earliest possible convenience."

"Today," says Klara.

Josef can't help but grin at the woman's cutting, stoic manner. "Today, then. Now, the sooner I'm allowed to finish with my client, the sooner I can tend to it."

The count peers from behind the changing screen.

"Yes, of course," Klara says. "Please, pardon my intrusion, Count Meusberger."

The count gives a nod, and Klara takes leave, followed by Anna, who manages a reserved but grateful glance at Josef.

FIVE

Of

LONGING

Anna chooses the room with the Stein fortepiano. As promised, Josef takes measures to ensure her comfort and privacy. First and foremost, the bed: a four-poster of dark mahogany with a tester from which hang rich, patterned curtains that can be drawn to enclose Anna within for warmth and seclusion. She rarely draws them, however, as she prefers to fall asleep to the warm glow of the fireplace and wake to the light of morning.

For concealment from the rest of the room, she instead makes use of an eight-paneled Coromandel lacquered screen. An inlaid mother-of-pearl scene depicts an ancient Chinese court. It is the most luxurious thing she has ever seen. Anna is humbly aware that Josef traded three of his clocks for it.

But if she considers any object divine, it is the Stein. Anna never touches the instrument, except to wipe it down every few days. Much more than a common harpsichord, she feels a person must earn the right to lay their fingers upon its keys, to caress melodies from its strings—a right earned from diligent practice and dedication, and passion.

Herr Künzi has that passion, of course. She hears it in his playing and sees it for her in his eyes. But heights make her nervous, and pedestals are merely things from which to fall. It is for that reason that Anna finds it difficult to reciprocate his feelings.

She's also reminded of a certain farm boy whose passion for God drew him away from her and to the seminary of Salzburg's Holy Trinity Church. Elias Dorn. She cringes at how easily his name and the devotion she had for him invades her memory. Then there's the clockmaker, who possesses so much passion for his work that one could say *it* possesses *him*. How silly she feels, that her longing for him seems to be a question waiting for an answer that never comes.

These are the wakeful longings that fill Anna's head one morning as she lies in her new bed behind the lacquered screen, the piano only feet beyond. The clockmaker has gone out on a walk. She does not feel a need to rise just yet. She stretches her arms upward and enjoys the texture of the covers against her breasts and her ribs, the weight of the linens like a gentle kiss. She massages her right arm downward to where it ends just above her wrist. The steel hand she wears is heavy and can leave her muscles stiff and fatigued.

She looks at the clockwork appendage at her bedside. It is both repulsive and beautiful; a horrific reminder of how she came to need it and a symbol of the care and benevolence she received from a stranger. Before that fateful night, she knew nothing of Josef Kronecker, and clocks were nothing more than utilitarian instruments that reminded her she was always late. She never considered their artistry. She never fathomed the life-giving possibilities that could be harnessed from the engineering of cold, lifeless materials.

Anna lays her head back, a peaceful heaviness to her eyes, and she floats back to a state that is not quite awake and not quite slumber. Then she feels the morning upon her face and imagines music from, at first, a faraway place. But soon it is upon her, infusing her morning.

She wakes fully to the realization that the music

is there in the room with her. Unaware of her presence behind the screen, someone is playing the piano. The melody is captivating yet unfamiliar. Too solemn for Mozart or Vivaldi. Too melodic for Bach. Anna searches for an appropriate description: a slow, lamenting sonata or adagio, in the lovesick key of C minor. The piece concludes with a sustained, hopeful G major chord that holds Anna as lovers do in the dawn. She stirs. The gentle rustle disturbs the quiet left behind in the music's absence.

"Herr Kronecker has a ghost?" comes the voice of Pascal Künzi.

Anna's own voice does not come, stilled beneath her now rapid breathing and racing heart. A part of her hopes he'll simply leave, while another part desires him to peer around the screen to discover her there, naked and warm. *What are you thinking?* she chides herself. Does she desire the young maestro, after all? Is she that desperate for the touch of someone—anyone?

"I have been called many things," Anna finally says, "but never a ghost."

She hears Pascal quickly stand. "Fräulein Klor?"

"No need to get up, Herr Künzi. This is where I

sleep now.”

“I’m sorry. I wasn’t aware. The door was open, and I let myself in.”

She smiles. Without seeing him, she guesses he blushes and averts his eyes.

“You couldn’t have known,” she tells him. “If you’ll allow me to get dressed, I’ll—”

A door closes on the other side of the screen. Anna listens closely for any sign of his presence. “Pascal?”

She giggles at the silence.

✦　✿　✦　✿　✦

Anna emerges from what is now her bedroom with the click of her cane upon the floor and finds Pascal amongst the clocks. Although embarrassed, he was impelled to stay in the shop. He cannot look at her. She conceals her impish grin with a cordial tone.

“Pascal, for what do I owe the pleasure of your visit this morning?”

“Please accept my apology, Fräulein.”

“Nonsense. You could not have been aware of my new sleeping arrangement. If I had known it came with such a beautiful melody to wake to, I would’ve moved in long ago."

Anna's lightness relaxes him, and he finally looks up. "Did you like it?"

"It was quite lovely, but I did not recognize it."

"It is my own composition—something I've been working on."

"Key of C minor, was it not? An interesting choice."

"You know music. Have you studied?"

"I've listened. My father played a pochette that he made himself. He would sing and play while the rest of us danced." Anna looks down at his left hand. Her forehead wrinkles.

"What is it?" he asks.

"I was just wondering how you could play something Herr Kronecker does not know."

"Something he has not made a disc for, you mean?"

"Yes."

Pascal raises his left arm. With his right hand, he adjusts the left thumb and pinkie finger slightly downward, separating them from the three middle digits. "With simple, perfect fifth chords." He demonstrates with a motion in the open air in front of him, as though playing a piano's lower register of keys.

This time, it is he who brings a smile to Anna's face, along with a laugh as welcome as the winter sun's warmth.

"I can never repay Herr Kronecker for what he's done," Pascal tells her, yet there's something else in his expression.

"But?"

"But I fear how long I will be able to carry on the charade."

Anna moves her cane to her right hand and places her left upon his arm. Her voice softens. "You must be one of the bravest men I know, Pascal."

He looks away. "I don't know that courage has anything to do with it."

"I do. I look forward to hearing your new work when it is done."

"That's why I've come here this morning, actually." He brightens. "I would like to extend an invitation to Herr Kronecker—and you—to see my performance in two weeks. My first since…"

"That's wonderful, Pascal."

He removes a formal invitation from his pocket. "It's being hosted by Duke Brunner. It should be quite the event. I plan to perform exclusively with a piano."

Anna's smile falters. "This event will be at his palace?"

"Yes," he answers, then embarrassment drains the pleasantry from the moment as he realizes how many stairs the duke's palace has. Too many to count. "I'm so sorry, Anna. I wasn't thinking."

"It's quite all right, Pascal. I forget my limitations myself, on occasion," she tells him but thinks: *No, I never forget. Ever.*

"You're kind—"

"How about you play your new work for me here when it is done? A personal performance." She gives him another reassuring touch. This time, her right hand to his left.

The tender humor of the gesture does not escape him.

✦ ❧ ✦ ❧ ✦

The palace of Leopold Brunner is humble by royalty

standards—a frustration for the duke, as humility was never part of his bloodline. He comes from a long line of arrogant Brunners, who attained aristocratic status by unsavory means and whose titles were mostly self-honorary.

The Brunner aristocracy—beginning in Southern Germany and spreading only as far as Northern Italy—has had little to no historical relevance in the grand scheme of aristocracies; the accumulation of whatever small territories they could acquire gave them little influence over greater affairs. Anytime war swept through the land, the Brunners willingly surrendered their holdings. Connivers and schemers, they were; soldiers and fighters, they were not. This, then, is the foundation upon which the current Duke Brunner's character is built.

His father, Renke Brunner, seeing his two sons as the last hope for the Brunner name, carefully plotted their future. For the eldest, Leopold, it would be a life of politics; for his younger brother, Gerhart, a pious path would be laid out to follow. It was Renke's theory that the family's history of mediocracy was due in part to never aligning themselves with the power of the

Roman Catholic Church. Like a dutiful pawn, Gerhart allowed himself to be wielded for sake of the family.

As for Leopold, he had no qualms living up to the legacy. The bribing of officials became as common to his nature as snow in the Alps. When those bribes—or *gifts*, as he liked to call them—were rejected by men of character, the duke was not beyond coercion or extortion to get what he wanted. Depending on one's social standing, Leopold Brunner was either a savvy politician or a spoiled tyrant.

Leopold's bullying, however, has mellowed in the wake of two critical events. The first was a heart attack, which brought to light the tenuous state of his health. The second was a woman. Anyone who knows the duke will agree that the best thing to ever happen to him was his much younger wife. Only sixteen when they married, she came from a modest background and gave the thirty-something Leopold devotion he never rightly earned. Where at first he was criticized for not marrying when he was younger, he was later lauded for not being rash and waiting for the perfect woman to join him. Other men now look upon her adoration for him with marvel and envy, while some women see her with a certain resentment, for she has not been burdened with the responsibility of having children.

Rumor has it (and we all know how nasty rumors can be), Leopold Brunner is unable to father children. He has commissioned—and decommissioned—many a physician in hopes of finding one who can come up with a satisfactory diagnosis and cure for his mysterious condition. The suggestion of having a surrogate step in to impregnate his wife was robustly dismissed.

"I'll not have bastard children around to remind me of my failure," was the duke's vehement proclamation.

Outside the entrance to the Brunner palace Josef Kronecker joins Dr. Baeder. It is the interior where the true opulence of royalty is evident: heightened columns and ornate carvings; polished floors of wood and marble; shimmering chandeliers; and many gold-framed mirrors, of which Josef comments, "One could argue their purpose is to spread the glow of candlelight. I find they are more in place to reflect the vanity of the residents."

After a bit of mingling, Josef and Christoph settle into a corner of the grand room from where they can watch other guests arrive. Christoph takes notice of the current women's fashion. They all wear corsets to achieve a flattened, tubular look.

"I fear a trend is developing and have considered doing a study on the ill effects of such a corset on a woman's health," Christoph says. "What it might do to their internal organs, being so compressed all the time...I foresee fainting due to the restriction of their breathing, issues with digestion, weakened back muscles."

While Christoph's theories would usually make for thought-provoking dialogue, it is only one woman in particular Josef is interested in thinking about or seeing. He has no reason to expect Klara, yet he hoped she might be here.

"Be careful, Josef," Christoph tells him. "Don't let obsession get the better of you."

"Obsession, you say?"

"And what would you call it, exactly?"

Josef takes a moment. "Mild curiosity."

Christoph laughs. "There is nothing mild about your curiosity. Tell me, in all earnestness, that your preoccupation with Klara has not been an infectious distraction these past few weeks."

"Infectious? So, I am no longer obsessed, but *infected* as well. Perhaps you should commit me to a hospital."

"That would be pointless, I'm afraid. Love is an incurable affliction. Perhaps an asylum would be more fitting."

Josef grins. "It seems I need a distraction, then, from my distraction."

"Indeed. Several, I would say."

So, distractions come. The first is Bishop von Bohn, whom Christoph and Josef espy mingling in the crowd.

"The duke's brother. I find it peculiar that he does not use the Brunner name." Christoph leans in and adds, "Also, I've heard that a scientific vocation was more fitting to his disposition than a theological one."

"One hears many things, if one wastes enough time in the company of mindless chatter." As the bishop starts in their direction, Josef adds, "I, for one, can't think of a more direct connection to God than through science."

"Herr Kronecker, isn't it? The clockmaker?" says

Bishop von Bohn.

"Yes, Your Excellency. How good to see you this evening."

"I've frequented your shop. I admire the work you do."

"You flatter me."

"I'm especially fascinated by the one rather large piece. Perpetual motion, is it not?"

"Your Excellency is very perceptive."

"I'd love to discuss it with you some time. Very fascinating."

"I'll be sure to make myself available the next time you're in."

Von Bohn's stoicism does not mask his innocent delight at the prospect. With a nod, he moves on from Josef and Christoph, and is soon replaced by the Marquis de Castile, Stefan Peiper. Another patient of Dr. Baeder's, Monsieur Peiper is a retired soldier; his last engagement was in the Austro-Turkish conflict. There, he suffered an injury from cannon fire that brought his military career to an abrupt end at the age of thirty-two. Christoph introduces the marquis to Josef.

"Dr. Baeder tells me you have skills beyond that

of master clockmaker," Stefan says.

"Yes," Josef replies. "I suppose that is true. It is a matter I prefer to discuss in the privacy of my studio, however."

"Oh, I understand. Would tomorrow be convenient for you?"

"I believe it would. Please join me for dinner. My assistant makes a delightful roasted duck."

A woman joins them and takes the marquis's arm. She is attired modestly. An embroidered, opaque veil of silk covers the upper area of her chest. A silken cap tops her raven-black hair. The outward fanning of her dress's hoop is far less ostentatious than commonly worn.

"Herr Kronecker," Stefan says, "my wife, Franziska."

Her behavior is reserved, as though she's holding something back. She and Josef exchange greetings. He can't help but notice the fervor within her dark eyes— so intense that he must look away out of gentlemanly courtesy to the marquis. She pulls herself close to Stefan, like a cat nuzzling its owner.

As the couple takes their leave, someone shouts

"Dr. Baeder!" from across the room. Leopold Brunner heads over to the doctor and the clockmaker, followed closely by two other gentlemen—on his right, a man with the face and manner of a small dog; to his left, one whose spindly legs strain to support the weight of his midsection that jostles in his effort to keep pace. The duke moves with great purpose. His height and bulk inspire the image of a ship cutting a path through the ocean.

"Dr. Baeder!" Brunner says again with boastful familiarity. "How good of you to come."

"An invitation I could not refuse," Christoph replies.

"One you *should* not refuse, I would say. I don't take kindly to rejection. Do I, Herr Weisman?" Leopold turns with a playful scowl.

The pointy, beady-eyed man standing close to the duke replies, "You have little patience for being refused. That is true, Your Grace."

"All in good humor, of course," the duke adds. "Gentlemen, let me introduce my consult and confidant, Matthew Weisman."

The men exchange cordialities.

"And my personal physician, Herr Klein."

The rickety man gives a pleased but tenuous nod.

Duke Brunner nods to Josef. "I believe this is the clockmaker you have spoken of, Herr Baeder. Josef Kronecker?"

Josef takes the duke's hand with a bow. "The honor is mine, Duke, sir. I am flattered and humbled to join you this evening."

"Thank our young musician for that. It was entirely his wish that you attend this performance. He, too, has spoken highly of you. Though I confess I am puzzled by the accolades placed upon mere time-pieces. A clock is a clock, is it not? But he, and the doctor here seem to find your work to be of great relevance."

"My friendship with Herr Künzi goes beyond 'mere' clockmaking," Josef patiently explains. "I'm a patron of his artistry, having followed his career for some years."

"He says you lent a critical hand in this return."

Josef maintains a serious expression. "Yes, you could say that."

"I'd be interested to know how, exactly."

"Another time, perhaps."

"Now would be the perfect time, I believe. If you wouldn't mind, Herr Kronecker?"

Before Josef can fabricate an explanation, Herr Künzi enters the room. With a sigh of relief, Josef says, "It seems our maestro has arrived."

All eyes are on the young musician now except for Leopold's, whose gaze lingers on the clockmaker a moment more. Being one whose word must be the last, he tells Josef, "Another time it will be, then."

Pascal approaches the stage at the center of the room to gentle applause—the kind that masks questions from his audience:

"Where has he been the past year?"

"Has he been of ill-health?"

"He appears much thinner, frail even."

No one else in the room waits with more tense anticipation than Josef. Pascal stands before the piano, then sits. Josef watches intently as the young musician takes in a deep breath and moves his right hand almost imperceptibly to his left. Only Josef knows it is to activate the appendage. Only Josef knows—just as he instructed him to—why Pascal pauses.

Then he begins to play.

As everyone else listens, Josef's attention is fully upon the young man's hands. As the right magically, effortlessly traipses over the keys, the left accompanies with steady precision. Or is it the right that follows the left, dutifully playing along as though keeping up with an unforgiving conductor? Only when he is satisfied that all attention is on Künzi and Leopold Mozart's C major Sonata, does Josef begin to relax.

On Pascal's face, there is no evidence of stress or panic—only the joy and contentment of playing once again before an audience. For a moment, Josef considers the unique challenge Künzi will face playing with other musicians, but soon, his thoughts are eclipsed by the lively sonata.

He takes in the myriad expressions as guests listen and enjoy.

Then there she is—Klara—smiling at him, not so much with her mouth, but with her eyes. The clockmaker reciprocates. Their encounter stops time. For one eternal instant, they are the only two in the room.

Applause breaks their spell, and Josef turns to see Herr Künzi now standing beside his piano. It seems he missed much of the evening's repertoire. The musician acknowledges the audience with a grateful bow as all stand in appreciation of his performance. Josef considers Anna's speculation—that perhaps the young musician's best future lies in being a one-handed virtuoso. Josef knows, one way or another, that Pascal will come to thrive on his own. But not yet. For now, he must emotionally and mentally heal, and Josef has been more than happy to aid the young man's transition.

As the ovation subsides, Josef stays back. Like a proud father, he allows others to gather ahead of him and give Pascal much-deserved accolades. He recognizes one patron in particular: Leopold Mozart, the composer of the performance's first selection, accompanied by a small child.

"What a joy to see you play again, Herr Künzi," Mozart tells Pascal.

"The honor is mine, sir." Pascal bows. "To have you attend this evening is a rare pleasure, indeed."

"I applaud your bold decision to perform with the pianoforte."

Pascal acknowledges the young man with Herr Mozart. "Who is this with you this evening?"

"This is my son Wolfgang." The boy, dressed quite formally, bows to Pascal with unexpected poise, giving him the appearance of a miniature adult. "He is only three but shows great interest and aptitude for music."

Pascal smiles. The boy smiles back.

As composer and musician converse, Josef feels a hand upon his shoulder and turns to find Klara. She says his name, and the whole of the palace burns from view in the light of her presence. "It's wonderful to see you," she tells him.

"You as well."

"It gives me a chance to apologize for my behavior when I saw you last. I have a tendency to speak on matters that are none of my concern."

"And I tend to be obtuse in regard to the circumstances of others. I should be thanking you, really. I believe Anna is quite enjoying her new accommodations."

"You believe?"

"Well, she has yet to say anything," Josef says a bit defensively. "We've been very busy."

Klara frowns. "I've done it again, haven't I?"

"There's no need to apologize. Unflinching concern for others seems to be in your nature. It's just one of your many charms."

The hint of a blush touches her cheek. "Many?"

"Countless."

Her blush is replaced by a teasing smirk that curls one corner of her mouth. "Perhaps you should know me better before you make such statements, sir."

Josef's chance to respond with his own flirtatious quip is interrupted by Christoph, who comes to stand beside them. "Klara, you *are* here."

"You were expecting otherwise, Dr. Baeder?"

"Well, someone was *worried* otherwise."

"Oh? Worried?" She turns to Josef.

He shakes his head. "I would not say *worried*."

"Concerned, then." Christoph grins.

"Concerned for what, exactly?" asks Klara.

"*Curious* is the word for which you two are desperately grasping. I was curious…" Pascal approaches, and Josef enthusiastically welcomes the interruption. "Klara, have you had the pleasure of meeting the honored guest? You will not find a finer musical artist than Herr Künzi."

"Of course we've met. Pascal, that was a magical performance. You've blessed us all with the opportunity to hear you play once again. Your time away served you well."

"The blessed opportunity was all mine." Pascal takes her hand with a bow. "I can't thank you enough. It was very generous of you to invite all these people into your home on my behalf, Duchess Brunner. I am forever grateful."

Josef and Christoph turn to each other, dumbfounded. Then, as fortuitous as a literary twist, the duke himself joins the group with his usual disconcerting exuberance.

"Herr Künzi, what a splendid performance, young man. Truly splendid."

Pascal bows. "You are too kind, sir."

Klara extends a hand to the duke. "Dr. Baeder, Herr Kronecker, let me introduce my husband, Leopold Brunner."

"Yes, we met earlier," Brunner says. "A most enjoyable conversation we had, in fact."

"Riveting, you might say." Christoph's sardonic undertone is fortunately lost on the duke.

Josef, on the other hand, is speechless. Awash with embarrassment and heartbreaking naïveté, he wishes he could be anywhere else at this moment. The others converse, but he doesn't follow what they say. Their words, their voices spin around him without sense or reason.

Christoph leans close. "I'm so sorry, my friend. I didn't know."

Heartbreaking, indeed. The clockmaker raises a hand to his chest.

"Josef." Klara peers at him. "Are you well?"

His vision blurs as blood drains from his head and clarity rushes from his consciousness. He sees himself as though from above and watches himself as his legs fold beneath him.

He collapses.

Christoph catches Josef before his head can hit the marble floor, then eases him down. "I need a room," he announces. "Somewhere private, so I can examine him."

"Of course," Klara says. "This way."

Two other gentlemen assist Christoph in carrying Josef. They follow the duchess to a sitting room. As soon as Josef is laid upon a sofa, Christoph ushers everyone away and closes the door.

"Christoph?" Josef manages.

The doctor hurries to his friend. "Yes, Josef. I'm here."

"It's…the…" Josef can't get the words out. He points a wavering finger to his chest.

Christoph opens Josef's jacket, his vest, and his shirt. Pinching the skin over Josef's heart, Christoph gives a hard tug and pulls back the flesh like layer, revealing a crystal box of gears and tubes where the clockmaker's heart should be. He places his hands on either side of the ticking pump and gently presses, peering into the intricate, glass-encased mechanism.

"It's the…main spring," Josef explains with a long exhalation.

"Are you sure you didn't just forget to wind it?"

"That's…part of the problem. It has required…more…winding lately. More often."

"When did you last wind it?" Christoph puts an ear to Josef's chest.

"Just before this evening's event. It should have lasted."

"It's pumping," Christoph concludes. "But it seems to be requiring extra effort to do so. Perhaps you've been under too much strain." He leans back. "You have the key?"

"Of course." Josef points to his vest pocket.

From it, Christoph removes a small clock key and inserts it into a hole beside the crystal box where Josef's left nipple used to be. He turns the key slowly. Though it's not the first time, reviving his old friend back to life remains a peculiar sensation.

The gears of the heart pump ever stronger with each turn of the key. Color returns to Josef's complexion, and the light of life brightens his eyes with each revitalizing pump. Josef lays his head back and breathes deeply. Clarity rushes to his head; vigor fills his body. Christoph listens again.

"We need to address this as soon as possible, Josef. You may not be so fortunate next time."

"I'm well aware. In fact, I recently completed an improved version. Christoph, you'll love it. It's *self-winding*."

With a frown, the doctor narrows his eyes.

"What?" Josef replies. "Are you not up to the

challenge?"

"It's not me I'm worried about. The last surgery nearly killed you. I worry how you'll fare a second time."

Josef gives a weak laugh. "I'd like to think your skills have improved as well as my design. You have the experience of having done it once before. No other surgeon can say that. And you cannot deny that all the walking I've been doing has made me fit as ever. Am I not the healthiest man you know…without a heart?"

Christoph laughs, then nods in apprehensive agreement. He places a hand on Josef's chest and watches the mechanized organ pump precious life through his body. "This is an amazing thing you've made, Josef. I can't wait to see the new one."

"Amazing?" comes Klara's voice from behind them. "*Miraculous* is a better word."

The two men turn to see her there with a full view of Josef's chest, his clockwork heart, and his greatest secret.

SIX

Of

SUMMER DAYS AND SLEEPLESS NIGHTS

Josef missed spring. Now, it is summer. But that's not to say the surgery took three months.

"In some ways, this procedure was easier than the first time," Dr. Baeder had explained to Anna after the operation.

"Because he already had a hole in his chest," she said.

"Exactly." Christoph laughed. "It was also fortunate that he had these issues, because the tubes we first used were deteriorating. They were near wearing through and preparing to leak. He would have bled to death, internally."

"His fortune is in having you as his physician."

Christoph ignored the compliment. "His age was a concern. Now, with the improved design of his new heart, he could very well outlive us all."

"You mean that it is self-winding."

"Yes. As long as he stays active, the heart will continue to pump."

"Like what's inside of Joop," Anna said. "That is why I must play with him once a day. So, his heart will never need to be rewound, then?"

"Only if he sleeps more than twelve hours. In this recovery period, he'll need windings twice a day, like before. Once he's up and around, though, perhaps just a few turns of the key in the morning will suffice."

With that, Christoph took a small key from his pocket and gave it to Anna. "One for you, of course."

She offered a slight smile. "I don't think he's ever slept more than a few hours a night."

"Don't for a moment think that he'll no longer need you, Anna. I'd say he needs you in his life now more than ever. I was joking when I said he may outlive us all. What's happened has only clarified his mortality. I don't think anyone should face that alone."

It was the initial recovery time that kept Josef from seeing the change of seasons. Dr. Baeder kept the clockmaker within the quiet seclusion of a private hospital room—one without a window. Aware of this,

Anna made sure that his room at home would allow for a variety of views.

From the window by his bedside, Josef can see the mountains in their summer splendor; through the other, he watches the town square and the city's day unfold.

One day, he spies a young girl selling flowers and asks Anna to buy him a bouquet for his room. Times of healing encourage altruism, and together, they decide to support the girl's livelihood by having her deliver an arrangement every day: purple-blue of gentian for the shop, red carnations and yellow arnica for Anna's room, and the star-like edelweiss everywhere else.

"We'll need more vases," says Josef. "Get some from Herr Eisenbein up the street. I imagine he could use the business."

The flower girl's visits become a regular part of the day, and she soon opens up and begins to share daily news off the street with Anna, who passes it on to Josef's delight.

As for Anna, she has been more than happy to drag herself up and down the stairs these days. Taking care of Josef has makes her feel less an assistant and more a caretaker or—dare she consider—a companion. Her efforts are not lost on Josef, either. He watches Anna as she works, how she goes along without complaint. Though she moves about with great labor, he can't help but admire her grace of spirit. Upon hearing the slow shuffle-thud-shuffle-thud of his assistant pulling herself up the steps to change his linens one afternoon, Josef emerges from his room to see her there, resting before she hauls herself upright.

"You really should hire someone to tend the upstairs," he tells her. "Perhaps the goldsmith's daughter from across the lane?"

Anna gives a tired but content smile. "No. I'm fine. Really."

"I think it's time, my dear, that I did something to improve the state of your legs. I can begin drawing up plans today."

There, at the top of the stairs, joy lights Anna's face like sunlight upon wild-flowers.

⊙ ❧ ⊙ ❧ ⊙

Anna's primary responsibility during Josef's recovery is keeping visitors at bay. Dr. Baeder is allowed, of course.

He comes on a daily basis to monitor his friend's recovery and engage him in backgammon. The other visitor she regularly allows in is Herr Künzi. At first, Josef feigns objection to the young man's presence. "You really needn't come by so often," he tells him. "I'm sure you have more pressing matters."

"What is more pressing than practicing? I can do that here as well as anywhere, can't I?"

Josef beams whenever Pascal plays. He soon stops pretending to object.

In rare circumstances, by Josef's insistence, Anna permits a client to call on the clockmaker for consultation. One such visit comes from Stefan Peiper, the Marquis de Castile, to whom Josef had promised an appointment the night of his collapse. After inquiring with sincere concern about the clockmaker's health, Monsieur Peiper paces nervously in front of Josef before finally explaining his needs.

"You may know that I had a distinguished military career."

"I do know that," Josef says. "An admirable career."

"Thank you. You may also know that it was

brought to a sudden end."

"The result of cannon fire, I was told."

"Yes." The marquis seems reluctant to continue.

Josef straightens in his chair, but remains quiet. The difficult nature of Stefan's experience looms thick in the room.

"I lost my genitalia," the marquis blurts. Then, silence.

Josef waits before offering, "I can only imagine the difficulties you've experienced as a result."

The marquis relaxes slightly, having shared his secret. "For myself, it is of little concern. A minor inconvenience. I can still perform all the necessary, natural functions. But you see…there's my wife, Franziska. You met her."

"Yes. I recall she was quite lovely."

"She has a simple beauty. I'll not deny that." His morose tone turns to one of zest. "But her *passion*. Oh, I will argue that few women could measure to that. And few men could resist her lovemaking. Most would trade their souls for one moment of intimacy with her."

Stefan falls quiet once again. Josef spies the glisten of a tear in the corner of his eye and tries to say what the marquis cannot: "Now you can no longer indulge in that passion."

Stefan's eyes widen. "No. No, it is not that, Herr Kronecker. I can indulge to my appetite's content. She insists upon that. But I cannot—I cannot satisfy *her* desires. I cannot fill her needs." The marquis locks his pleading gaze on Josef.

"If I am understanding you," Josef says, "you're asking me to make an object for sexual purposes." He pauses. "Objects designed for a woman's pleasure are not unheard of. But I sense that you would prefer something you could wear during times of intimacy. An extension of your passion, your love for Franziska. Is that correct?"

For the first time since their meeting, a smile comes to Stefan's face.

"You have no difficulties otherwise with any of the normal functions of that area?" Josef asks.

Stefan wipes his eyes. "None."

"Give me a couple of weeks, Monsieur Peiper. And be assured, I will use the utmost discretion in this matter."

With a nod, the marquis takes Josef's hand.

Anna's greatest challenge is Klara, whose determination makes for a worthy rival. Although the duchess was responsible for Anna's new accommodations, she does not have a warm spot for nobility. In fact, she is quick to distrust anyone of royal standing. She finds them all suspect.

"How is he doing today?" Klara inquires on her first visit. "May I see him?"

"He's asleep," Anna tells her.

The next day, the duchess asks with the warmest tone, "I'd very much like to talk to him, if I may?"

"By Dr. Baeder's orders, he's not to be disturbed."

The more Klara persists, the more Anna enjoys resisting.

"I've brought him some pastries." Klara holds a sweetly decorated tin. "Fruit-filled, with a hint of rum. Delectable."

"He is on a very strict diet at the moment." Anna takes the tin. "But perhaps I could sneak one to him later."

Klara returns the following day with a different strategy. Before Anna can turn her away, the duchess tells her, "I would like to buy a clock."

"Oh?"

"Yes, there are so many lovely pieces here. How could I not?"

Anna pauses, having been taken off guard. "Who is this purchase for?"

"For myself. I could use one for my bedroom." Klara looks about the shop. "But, I've no idea where to start. Perhaps you could assist me?"

"Well," Anna begins, "I am unfamiliar with the décor of your room, but I imagine pieces like these would not do." She motions to a collection of mantel clocks, each case made of a dark wood that is either polished or lacquered. "While they are contemplative, they lack humor."

"You find me humorous?"

"Not of frivolity, madam. You have a thoughtful, perceptive wit. A very becoming trait."

The duchess nods a gracious "thank you."

Anna continues amongst the displays. She stops occasionally to lean upon her cane and consider the inventory. Looking to a row of porcelain and crystal clocks, as colorful and glimmering as an Austrian hillside after a spring rain, Anna shakes her head. "Too delicate." She peers down another row, this one lined with longcase pieces as immense as eight feet. "Quite ostentatious, actually. They lack your demure."

"How about this one?" Klara points to a clock the size and shape of a small royal scepter. The assortment of metals, colors, and intricate designs that make up its case detract from the diminutive hands and numerals of its dial.

"If you're a courtesan, perhaps," Anna replies. "It is more decorative than functional. You'd want to know the time at a glance, without the inconvenience of having to look too hard, wouldn't you?"

"True."

Anna moves to a table where a piece with a pair of bronze figurines—a woman and a man—sits. They lie beside a sublime clockface made of pearl, gold hands, and ebony Roman numbers. The woman wears a flowing, seductive chemise and reclines against the clockface while her suitor kneels beside her, fawning for her attention. But she looks away from him. She is either teasing him by feigning disinterest or disregarding him outright, having neither the inclination nor the time for what he has to offer. Either way, the poor fellow is at her mercy.

"I recommend this one," Anna tells the duchess.

Klara leans in, then steps back. A grin parts her lips. Without a word, the duchess saunters back to the row of longcases. "I do like this one," she says, standing before a six-foot-tall piece. Its case is oak with walnut veneer, and its panels are olive wood marquetry the likes of which the Duchess has never seen: ivory, green-stained bone and a variety of fine woods. With an admiring sigh, Klara adds, "Such understated stature and noble presence. Like…"

"A queen?"

"An empress."

Anna doesn't say, but it has long been one of her personal favorites. She looks at Klara, feeling for a moment like a forlorn figurine at her feet, and realizes the duchess is not one to be trifled with. "I'll have it delivered first thing tomorrow."

Klara returns to the shop days later, thinking her purchase of the clock was an act of good faith. She carries a bouquet of heather for Josef.

Anna immediately turns her away. "Oh, I'm afraid he'll have such a reaction to those, and sneezing or coughing must desperately be avoided."

Klara scrutinizes the shop blooming with gentian and edelweiss.

Anna responds with, "No heather, as you see."

Klara retreats once again.

One day, Anna finds herself confronted with a customer as disconcerting as the duchess. He enters the shop late in the morning. At first, she thinks it is Bishop von Bohn, seeing him only from behind. But upon closer examination of the black, robe-like zostikon and the black, embroidered skufia atop his head—the distinctive clothing of a priest—Anna realizes it is not. Her stomach tightens. Except for the stoic but pleasant Bishop von Bohn, the only men she has greater disdain for than those of royalty are those of the cloth *in persona Christi*. The sight of the priest reminds her of how she came to be in Salzburg and the turbulent turn her life took.

It began with the young Elias Dorn, whose eyes

were the color of a lake before winter. His blond hair fell to his shoulders. Not just any shoulders, for God's sake, but those of a hard-working farm boy.

For God's sake, indeed.

It was for God that he went away. It was in Christ that he found his calling.

"You found Christ?" she had teased him.

"Yes."

"I didn't know he was lost," she added, naïve to the gravity of his decision. A choice, she would learn, that rested heavily upon those shoulders.

"I must go," he told her with all seriousness. And go he did to the seminary of Salzburg's Holy Trinity Church to wear the clothes of a presbyterate.

She followed in hopes of finding him and convincing him otherwise, only to endure horrors that eventually dropped her into the hands of a benevolent clockmaker and led her to this very moment, seeing a priest in Kronecker's shop, and being assaulted by memories she had futilely tried to suppress.

"Can I help you?" Anna manages to ask the priest after a deep breath.

"Oh, yes, I'm looking for a gift." He examines an

oak grandfather clock.

She moves closer. "Did you want something so large? Or would you prefer a smaller, more personal piece like those to your left there?"

Taking her advice, he eyes a shelf of mantel clocks. "These are lovely."

"Who is this for, if I may ask?"

"My teacher."

"How would you describe him, in a single word?"

He straightens his broad shoulders, intrigued by the question. "Stately."

Anna moves yet another step closer. "And how would you describe your relationship with this stately gentleman?"

"He's been like a father to me." The priest finally turns to face her.

Anna stops breathing. All her weight sinks onto her cane. If she could find her voice, she would say: *How do you think own your papa, Meinhardt, would feel about that?*

Or she might scream. But all she can manage is a faint, "Elias…"

His forehead creases with puzzlement. "Yes?"

She struggles to contain the vehement eddy of

repugnance and outright hatred churning inside her.

Then he recognizes her. "Annamarie?" His face contorts into a smile, then a frown and a confused pause. "What are you doing…here?"

The thorny lull is enough for her to gather herself. "I work here. I am Herr Kronecker's assistant."

"What I mean is—"

"I know what you mean."

"What happened to you? I didn't recognize you."

She regains her balance and moves neither toward him nor away, but laterally before him.

He smiles again, genuine yet wary. "It's good to see you."

"Is it? I wish I could say the same." She now gives the priest a look so cold and spiteful it flattens his smile, drains the color from his face, and snuffs the glint in his eyes.

"You didn't have to come here. I didn't ask you to. You should have stayed home."

"It is you who should have kept your promise."

With an arrogant lift of his chin, he replies, "I did. But a much greater promise than the one you think I made to you."

At another time in her life, such a statement would have broken Anna. But now, it is nothing compared to what she's since endured. She lifts her head as well and makes her way to the black, gold-trimmed mantel clock the bishop had his eye on. That she moves assisted by a cane does not escape Elias's attention.

"What has happened to your legs?"

"I'm guessing this gift is for Bishop von Bohn."

"Yes. As a matter of fact—"

"This is what you're looking for. A timepiece for a stately father figure."

Elias awkwardly looks the clock over, taking in the details as Anna watches him. Finally, he says, "It's perfect."

"I'll hold it for you until you can send someone to pick it up, along with payment. Or I can arrange to have it delivered to you."

"I'll return to pick it up next week."

"I would rather you didn't. I'd prefer you send someone else. It would bring me great pleasure to know that, when you leave now, I shall never see you again."

Elias's mouth tightens and he turns from her. "Good day, Annamarie."

"Goodbye."

A series of sleepless nights plagues Josef. On one in particular, he wanders to the workroom. He finds Joop and hefts the mechanical lad down from his perch. He stands him up and opens the back of his shirt, checking the slot and lever for any encumbering debris. Josef reaches for the box of metallic discs, removes one, and inserts it into the slot. He flips the lever.

Joop walks. With an uncanny sense of balance in his youthful stride, the automaton wanders about the backroom. He exhibits an eerie familiarity with the space. The ballerina in Vienna had been impressive, but her human-esque qualities paled in comparison to Josef's creation. From the muscular tension of the legs and the swing of the arms, to the playful, inquisitive twitch of the fingers, Joop is the clockwork embodiment of a living, breathing boy. Even his chest expands and contracts in the simulation of breaths. A passerby could look into the shop and truly believe the clockmaker was in the company of a child. Until, however…Josef frowns at the sight of the empty eye-sockets.

He starts when Anna comes up behind him.

"It seems insomnia is contagious," he says.

"Is there anything I can get for you?" she asks.

"I did have a thought…"

"Yes?"

Josef places another disc into the boy and begins to play pat-a-cake with him. "It has been some time since I asked you to get eyes for Joop. I was just wondering."

"I have yet to find the right crystals," Anna explains. "Then there's been the matter of your recovery." Joop give the clockmaker a hug. "I have been wondering, too, in fact…"

"Yes?"

"Well, I have an idea about a source for the perfect stones, but it would require I be more mobile than I am."

"I see," Josef says, continuing to pat with Joop as he speaks. "I've drawn plans and ordered parts to improve your situation. It shouldn't be much longer."

Anna's smile is a mere shadow of the glee she feels at hearing that. She watches Josef with Joop, noticing that with each round of pat-a-cake, the clockmaker hugs the toy a little tighter.

Later that morning, Anna mentions Josef's sleeplessness to Christoph, adding, "He's been spending a great deal of time with Joop. More than normal."

The doctor gives the matter careful consideration before answering. "I have him on a fairly low dose of laudanum for pain, but even in small amounts, the tincture can cause hallucinations, vivid dreams, or nightmares."

"I wonder what kind of imaginings could cause him such restlessness."

"I am no philosopher of psychology. From what you say, I would venture to guess he's been thinking of the carriage accident."

"Carriage accident?"

Christoph nods once. "Yes. The carriage accident—that killed his wife and child some years ago."

Anna stops in mid-breath. Her eyes widen.

"He's not told you about that?" Christoph asks.

"We…don't have that kind of relationship."

"I'm sorry. I thought you knew."

"What happened?"

"The coachman was driving too fast. The carriage overturned and careened down a hillside. I'd like to think they were killed right away, without suffering, but it was some time before the accident was discovered. Josef has been convinced—tortured, by the thought—that if only someone had found them sooner…"

"If only someone had been walking by," Anna adds with a faraway gaze. *What a bastard fate can be.*

Christoph puts a gentle hand on her shoulder. "Yes. If only."

That afternoon, as Christoph accompanies Josef in his study, he does not bring up the subject of sleepless nights. Instead, Josef consults him about a current project—the phallus for the Marquis de Castile. Because who better to understand male and female genitalia and the sexual needs of a woman than a physician?

"Well," Christoph holds the initial wax form in his hand, "it seems to be of appropriate circumference and length."

"Not too large or too small?"

"No. I wouldn't think that size matters much, actually. It certainly needn't be larger." The doctor gives a wink.

Josef chuckles, but his brow furrows thoughtfully. "Maybe smaller, then?"

Christoph wraps his hand around the object. "No, this should do fine. However…"

"Yes?"

"I think some texture would be appropriate. To best replicate the sensation for her."

Josef makes a note.

"And make sure it is a circumcised representation."

"Of course," Josef agrees, then adds, "I've considered designing it to hum or vibrate."

"Why?"

"I thought the marquis might enjoy the sensation—a mutual connection during coitus."

The doctor taps his chin with a finger. "I've read of something called a tremoussoir. It's a vibrating device strictly for the treatment of hysteria in women. I suppose it could add a simple pleasure to the experience."

"Well, it's something I'm thinking about."

Josef makes more notes, giving Christoph a moment to further examine the model. "It's a shame," he says, "that you can't find someone who could try out your design."

The two men look at each other, grin, then break into a ribald laugh.

⊕ ⚬ ⊕ ⚬ ⊕

Josef is not the only one suffering restless nights. Anna has become haunted by a deep longing for the touch of another. From someone. Anyone. The need overwhelms common sense or propriety; fantasies infiltrate her sleep. She imagines hands upon her in the dark of night that veils her deformity. She cannot see this dream-lover's face. She only feels him. His touch upon her. His flesh inside her.

This faceless incubus moves upon her, and she moves her hands over him. She molds him after the men in her life. She caresses the scars of the clockmaker's chest. She takes hold of the lean arms of the pianist. She digs her nails into the broad shoulders of the priest. When she reaches the peak of her throes, Anna shudders into pieces. A hand falls off here. An arm there. Legs detach lifelessly to the floor. An eye pops out.

She wakes with a jolt to sopping sheets.

Anna struggles from her bed and puts on a chemise. Josef is up in his room, so she allows herself to wander freely about the shop in hopes of calming her carnal malaise. It doesn't help that she still thinks of the clockmaker and then the maestro. Her lust still lingers.

It isn't until Elias Dorn—the farm boy-cum-priest—enters her mind that Anna's amorous feelings begin to wane.

He may have come to her in her dream, but her waking memory of Elias is not about desire or a broken heart. She looks down. What was once her right hand is now a mechanism of tempered steel designed for the simple task of grasping. A thought comes to her: *I could use it to grasp his throat and squeeze.* She is reminded of what became of her through every waking moment of her life, from struggling out of bed in the morning to each effortful step she takes before collapsing from exhaustion at night. Anna can never forget.

She finds herself in the clockmaker's study. The room is dimly lit by a single candle; Josef has gone and forgot to extinguish the light once again. She knows she should leave and lock the door behind her, but Anna looks about the darkened room as though peering into the deep recesses of Josef's imagination. She gazes upon the table of schematic sketches, which read to her like ancient hieroglyphics. She gawks at designs she hopes will help her walk and parts of prototypes and pieces to puzzles that he will construct into who-knows-what.

Anna spots a collection of paintings she's never noticed before. They lean against the wall behind the worktable as though haphazardly stashed away to be forgotten for another time. Or forever.

She's about to grab the candle to take a closer look at the artwork when she spies something else on a nearby shelf: an object sitting upright that appears to be an eight-inch shaft with a diameter a little over an inch. She takes a closer look. It is an impressive likeness, but she cannot imagine what it would be doing in Josef's study. Anna finds herself impelled to touch it.

The surface is smooth, yet it has some texture—circular ridges that spiral around the length of it. It narrows slightly toward the top, but then is capped with a kind of mushroom-shaped knob. Anna wraps her fingers around it—not too tight—and exhales, then inhales while moving her hand down the ribbed shaft and back up again.

She has an idea.

Josef returns to his study as the sun comes up and finds a hot chocolate awaiting him. He is unaware his assistant has slept as little as he, deceived how refreshed she appears as she wishes him a pert, "Good morning."

The clockmaker is not so fresh. The weight of his work and his recovery rests heavily upon him. He looks at her with equal parts envy and scorn as she departs. When she returns to his study a few minutes later, another cup of chocolate in hand, she lingers.

"Yes?" he asks.

"You left your studio unlocked last night," she tells him. "I locked it for you."

"Oh? Well, thank you." He turns back to his work, but Anna mills about the room. "Was there something else?"

"You've solicited suggestions from me about your designs in the past, have you not?"

"Yes, of course. Your insights have often helped."

She looks for the right words.

"What is it?" he asks.

Her eyes move from him to the shelf beside her and the object he's made for the Marquis de Castile.

"This phallus…"

"Yes? What about it?"

"It seems to me," Anna continues, "that it requires some manner in which it can be heated. Perhaps a chamber within which hot water could be poured, to better replicate body temperature."

Then she turns and leaves.

Josef looks at the steel penis, taking her suggestion under consideration as he experiences one of his more obtuse moments, for he does not—not even for a second—think about how she might have come to such a conclusion.

SEVEN

Of

THINGS ONCE LOST

Anna should have seen the *Schnürlregen*—or "rain in strings"—of the summer months as an omen.

When the sun finally comes out, she takes the opportunity to sweep the cobblestones in front of the shop. Mornings like this usually make her a little less unhappy. It is on this morning, however, that Dr. Baeder arrives with the Duchess Brunner on his arm.

"Good morning, Anna," Christoph says.

Klara gives her a knowing nod—knowing, of course, that she has won—and an ever-so-demure and victorious smirk. Anna is left with nothing to do but watch them parade past and enter the shop. So engrossed is Anna that she doesn't notice the approach of Bishop von Bohn until he speaks. She turns to the cheerful cadence of his normally stolid speech.

"Your Excellency?"

"Good morning, Fräulein," he repeats. "Are you well?"

She feigns a smile. "How could I not be on a morning like this?"

"It is especially lovely, isn't it?"

Anna moves to allow the bishop into the shop, but he remains in place with a raised hand.

"I haven't time today," he tells her. "I just wanted to thank you. For the clock."

"It was your priest that purchased it for you, not I."

Von Bohn laughs. "Young Dorn may be theologically astute and zealous in his devotion, but his artistic sensitivities tend to be a bit commonplace, if not cliché. Left to his own proclivity, he would have given me an enormous grandfather clock or something equally—"

"Cloddish?"

"Oh, so you know him?"

Anna shares a laugh with the bishop like she has not done with anyone for a very long time. In that moment, on that sun-filled morning, the circumstances that dictate her life fade to triviality. Elias Dorn?

Duchess Brunner? *To hell with them.*

🕐 • 🕑 • 🕒

Christoph knows all too well how involved Josef becomes in his work, and so he makes his way to the study accompanied by Klara with a playful grin upon his face. The clockmaker's back is to the door when they enter. Christoph does not wait to be acknowledged for he knows how long that could take.

"Josef, I need to speak with you."

Josef keeps working.

"There is something of great urgency I need to ask you."

No response.

"See?" Christoph tells Klara, loud enough for the clockmaker to hear. "Just as I said."

When Josef still fails to respond to their presence, Klara grows tired of the game and says, "Hello, Josef."

He looks up but not around. The voice transports him back to when he first heard it in the home of the Altbrussers' on that fateful night.

Klara steps farther into the study. "How is your

heart?"

Josef finally turns and sees her, as resplendent as ever. He pauses, then says, "Duchess Brunner."

"Oh," replies Klara with a wry smile, "so formal."

"You are a duchess, are you not? Married to Duke Leopold Brunner?"

Her smile fades. "Yes, that is true." She steps closer still, not once averting her eyes from him. "How are you doing? You look well."   "I've lost a good deal of weight."

"It suits you."

"My doctor recommends I eat as much as I like—a prescription to which I have no objection."

Christoph takes a moment to examine Josef. All the while, Klara locks her eyes upon the clockmaker, who finds he couldn't look away if he wanted to. Satisfied, Christoph tells him, "I hope you don't mind. I thought it would be good if the two of you spoke."

Christoph leaves them. Klara breaks gaze her and looks around the room. She walks as she takes in all the details without lingering on any one thing too long. Josef welcomes the respite from her close proximity and holds his place.

"What are you working on now?" she asks. "A mechanical breathing apparatus? A clockwork liver, perhaps?"

"A sphincter," he replies with grave seriousness—a tone that puzzles Klara.

"Sphincter?"

"For politicians and the like to wear over their faces in hopes of regulating the constant flow of excrement from their mouths."

Klara lets go with a laugh that thins the tension in the room. "May I listen?" she asks. "To your heart."

Josef shrugs. "If you must."

Klara moves close to him. She turns her head and leans in to put an ear to Josef's chest. He breathes in the fragrance of her wig and the marjoram flowered aroma of her skin. He resists with every bit of his weakened state the urge to touch the nape of her neck or run his fingers along her partially bare shoulder. Klara looks up, her face now closer to his than it has ever been.

"I didn't know if what I had seen was true or not," she tells him.

Her breath mingles with his. She places a hand upon his chest and feels the mechanism within pulsate beneath her fingertips. She takes in the lines of his face and how the years have carved it so distinguishably.

"It's amazing."

They are now near enough to kiss.

Josef backs away. He meets the edge of his worktable, slides along it until he comes to a chair at one end, and settles upon it in a slump.

"I'm sorry, Josef."

"I blame myself. It was silly of me to think a woman like you would have been without a husband."

While Klara no longer blushes at such compliments, she does smile.

"Yet," Josef adds, "being *a duchess* is a detail one tends not to omit from conversation."

"The title is not one I would have chosen for myself. But it was important to my father. His dying wish, you might say. I loved my father and was not going to disappoint him. As for myself, I wish for people to know me as I am, not for my title."

"It is not only your title to which I am referring."

Klara concedes with a sigh. "Our meeting in Vienna was merely circumstance. You see—I was looking for a lover, not love. You might say it's a game

I enjoy. Maintaining an air of anonymity is part of the arousal for me."

"I see. And what is the duke's opinion of your game?"

"He allows me my indulgences. He finds them trivial, as do I."

"I see."

"However, this time it was not so trivial. I misled myself as well as you. It's difficult for me to admit that I could be drawn to another man as much—or *more*—than my husband. Again, I apologize."

Josef straightens in his chair. "Your apology is not exactly helping."

She looks to his chest once more. "It's an extraordinary thing you've done, Josef." Her eyes meet his again. "Truly extraordinary."

"I should say the same of you, my dear."

"Oh? How so?"

"To have given a man without a heart such debilitating emotions."

She longs to take him.

"I think it's time you left," he tells her.

Klara's expression says otherwise, yet she

concedes. "Take care, Josef."

"Good day, Duchess Brunner."

۞ ❧ ۞ ❧ ۞

Klara returns to the palace to find her husband's physician, Herr Klein, being escorted from the premises with a slumped, dejected posture. He manages a pleading look to as he passes in hopes she'll do something to help his situation, but she does nothing but watch him exit with calculating concern. Herr Weisman enters the foyer next, as though on cue, to address her questioning glare.

"It seems the duke is dissatisfied with yet another doctor," Weisman says. "How many is that now? Five? Six?"

The duchess doesn't answer.

Weisman counts upon his fingers. "Oh, no. It's *seven*." He gives her a taunting grin. "In the whole of the medical profession, there must be a physician somewhere who can unveil the mystery of the duke's inability to father a child. Whatever will he do?"

Klara turns from Weisman without a word. Before turning, however, she gives him a look that suggests he should follow her—or else. In the adjacent library, the duchess waits for the duke's confidant to enter and close the door behind him.

"I've asked you before," Klara begins with restrained vehemence, "to keep your opinions on this matter to yourself. If you have something you must say to me, do so in private."

"Not an opinion, madam. Merely an observation."

"In the future, make your observations in silence. They are of little use to me."

"Very well, madam." Weisman bows. "I do have one concern…"

"Yes?"

"What will you do when your husband commissions a doctor who possesses the kind of character and integrity that cannot be seduced?"

"*If* he finds such a man, you mean."

"You know he will. Eventually. Which begs the question: what will he do to *you* when your secret is revealed? Much more than simply having you escorted from the palace, I imagine."

Klara takes a step forward. "You know very well

what he will do to me. The same thing he will do to you for your complicity."

Herr Weisman gives her a patronizing nod—a wordless "touché." As she moves past him toward the door, he can't help but add, "Speaking of men of integrity, the duke has considered offering Dr. Baeder the position."

She stops and considers his statement. "Now, *that* is something of use to me."

Exactly why Elias Dorn is returning to Kronecker's shop two weeks later, even he can't explain—only that he is determined to see Anna again. It is early morning, before Anna has opened the door for business. He taps lightly upon the glass. Then a little harder. She emerges from behind the black curtain at the back of the shop.

Anna sees him through the glass, wide-shouldered and reserved, and makes her way to the front door, wondering all the while if she shouldn't. She meant it when she said she never wanted to see him again. But here he is. Her curiosity gets the best of her with every burdensome step. Not once does she avert her eyes from his solemn grin or pitying gaze—the very look he gave her when he left the first time so long ago. She unlocks and opens the door, then forces Elias into an excruciating moment of silence. She takes pleasure in giving him nothing.

He musters a feeble, "Good morning, Anna. I wonder if I might speak with you?"

She turns away with an impassive roll of her eyes. "Be sure to close the door all the way, so it stays latched."

He follows her slow gait and takes notice of the common servant's apron she wears. "I apologize for this early call. Seeing you the other day has brought on sleepless nights."

"I've had a few of those myself of late." She stops without facing him. "But not because of you."

"Of course. I imagine creating these beautiful pieces would keep one's mind rather occupied."

"Taking care of—" Anna begins. Then, "*Assisting* Herr Kronecker can be consuming, yes. So consuming, in fact, that you'll not mind if I continue my work while you have your say."

He follows her to the back of the shop. She pulls

aside the black curtain and stops to see that she secured the door to the menagerie before allowing Elias to enter, then she resumes her morning routine.

Elias stands just inside the doorway. He gathers his thoughts before beginning. "Anna, seeing you the other day was a…shock…a surprise. A very pleasant surprise, of course."

She straightens a set of tools.

"I must admit that I honestly never expected to see you again. Ever. Especially here in Salzburg."

She organizes a bin of gears.

"You always spoke about a home in Hallstatt, a house by the lake." An awkward smile crosses his face.

She dusts a shelf.

His smile fades. Sadly but firmly, he says, "Anna, please."

She turns to him with a gaze of such contempt that he questions whether or not he should continue.

But he does. "I've come to speak with you. And if you wouldn't mind, I'd appreciate it if you didn't work. For a moment. For what we once had."

"For what we once had?" Her gaze intensifies. "What about for what we could've had? For what you promised me?"

"You place too great a value on the promises of youth."

"No. I placed too great a value on promises from *you*."

Elias's shoulders slump beneath her blow, but he bounces back and raises them even higher than before. "I answered my calling. I couldn't ignore it. I don't apologize for it, Anna. I am not sorry for my love of God and the work I do for Him."

She teeters. His arrogant proclamation fans the ire she's kept to a smolder for so long. "My mother and father love God, as did yours, yet they love each other just as well, and their children. They work, side-by-side, and love the life they've made together just as much as God." Her rising emotions take her off balance. Elias reaches out a hand to help, but she slaps it away with her cane. "Have you forgotten your family, Elias?"

"I am devoted to something greater than the life to which you aspire. You never understood, Anna. It seems you never will."

Her breaths become shallow and rapid; she is a kettle on the verge of boiling. "It's you who doesn't understand. You have…no idea." She moves into better light. "I followed you, Elias. That's how I came to be here in Salzburg. I came after you, to bring you back home with me."

"I didn't know…"

"Of course you didn't. I never found you. But I did find cruelty. Unimaginable cruelty. All because I was too foolish to leave Salzburg without you. Because of my stubbornness. Because of *my devotion* to you."

Elias is so caught up in Anna's narrative that he does not notice she is untying the strings of her apron as she speaks.

"I found work in the vocation of servitude," she continues. "It is good work, is it not, to serve others? *God's* work?"

She removes her apron.

"But they were demons I served. Men who wanted more from my body than hard work. When I refused, I was beaten."

She unclasps her bodice.

"I never stayed long enough to learn what would happen if I denied a master's urges a second time. Instead, I found another master. And another. Each of them worse than the one before…"

Now she begins to tug at the "flesh" that covers her right hand.

"…until I met Satan himself. And I couldn't escape, no matter how hard I fought."

Anna unrolls the skin-like material of her forearm.

"I struck him hard, clawed his face with my right hand while he held down my left." A bitter smile parts her lips. "I can only hope he still has the scars."

"Anna?" Elias utters as he watches her pull the glove, inch-by-inch, from the cold steel underneath.

"To keep me from clawing him again, he broke it." She raises her hand, in all its mechanized glory, into plain view. With a twitch of her shoulder, she snaps the fingers open and then closed. "It's hideous and beautiful at the same time, is it not?"

Elias leans forward. "It is…miraculous."

Anna snorts. "Funny you choose that word. But, yes, it is a miracle. A man-made miracle."

"I'm so sorry, Anna, for what you've suffered."

Elias's sympathy is genuine. So heartfelt, in fact, that sorrow threatens to swell within Anna. She closes her eyes and tightens her mouth to keep the tears at bay. "Oh, Elias. This is not…no, that was only the beginning. With my hand broken, the beast was determined as ever to mount me. But I kicked at him. You remember how strong my legs were? I kicked at him with everything I had to keep him off of me, and *out* of me. Until he called for help. Then, with more hands to hold me down—"

"He raped you."

Anna looks at Elias with a distant gaze. "Oh, no. No. He broke my legs. He crushed my beautiful, strong legs. With his fists and his feet. With a bust of Descartes. He even made a joke. 'That should enlighten her,' he said and laughed. His men laughed. I could do nothing but lie there, immobilized."

A tear rolls down Elias's cheek.

"And *then* he raped me."

A dry swallow gags the priest.

"It took less than a minute for him to satisfy his carnal desire. When he was done, do you know what he said?"

Elias shakes his head.

"Throw her away."

All this while, as she spoke, Anna slipped off her

bodice. She now holds her dress loosely around her.

"So, they did, but not before having their own way with me, of course. It'd have been a shame to let me go to waste. When they were done, they hauled me to the nearest ravine. It was there that they tossed me away. I slid down the shale like it were ice and onto the rocks at the bottom. My head landed against a stone with such force"— Anna *slaps* the side of her head—"it left me cockeyed on this side. Have you even noticed, since you've seen me again, how this eye does not align with the other?"

Elias stands mute.

"It doesn't matter," Anna continues. "I was left for dead. I would have surely died if—"

"If God hadn't been with you."

"What did you say?"

"God was with you. He had a plan for you and wasn't going to let you die."

A morgue-like silence chokes the air between them. The clocks seem to stop.

"*God?*" Anna cries from the darkest depth of her anger. "Are you telling me God did this?" She lets her dress drop to the floor. Elias stumbles backward, away from the woman disrobed before him. What is left, that is, of the woman before him.

The dull metal of her hand he found miraculous a moment ago loses its wonder beside the hard, gray steel that takes the place of her missing legs. Stunning in their technology, terrifying in their dehumanization. In marvel and repulsion, the simple-minded priest stares at each intricate gear and spring and wire. He takes in every inch of the mechanized limbs. From the claw like feet, to the hinged ankles, steel-framed calves, and clockwork thighs.

With a gasp and another step back, Elias moves his astonished gaze up her artificial limbs to where they meet an artificial pelvis. He scrutinizes the glistening surface of porcelain and finds the legs are attached to a deep, formfitting urn within which Anna's torso rests. It's as white as her skin, making it difficult to tell where the vessel ends and the flesh of her abdomen begins.

He falls, tripping over himself to the floor at the realization that Anna is naked before him. The steel of her appendages blurs. Her bare form seems to float, suspended in air. Her stomach, her arms, her shoulders. How her auburn hair falls against her neck. Her breasts, heaving at him. The priest struggles to his feet and draws Anna fully into focus. The cruel steel of her hand and legs. The pure white glass of her artificial pelvis. Her very real flesh. His heart races. Not with lust, but with horror.

"What have they done to you? They turned you into…"

"Into what, Elias?"

"You're a monster."

Now Anna is the one in shock. "A monster?"

"Look at you."

"Herr Kronecker and Dr. Baeder saved my life. They found me and pulled me from the rocks, as near to death as one can get."

With a thrust of her hips and a push with her cane, Anna gives the legs a brief life of their own. They propel her forward, two, three, four steps. Elias watches, terror stricken.

"To save what little life I had left, my hand and legs were removed. Dr. Baeder kept the rest of me alive, while Josef—a mere clockmaker—worked countless days and nights to give me…" Anna looks down at herself. She touches, almost seductively, the metal that is her thigh, and upward to the glass vessel in which her body rests. "He had to make this for me because the original leather straps rubbed me raw. It was the best he could do, he told me, to bring steel and flesh together. He said its surface matched my skin." With a teasing, wicked giggle, she caresses herself upward, her fingertips tracing the lines of her body. "It does, don't you think?"

Elias's eyes dart about in search of the way out of the shop.

"I am a miracle, Elias. Not a monster. I am a marvel of man's ingenuity. God was not there when I was beaten. He was not watching while I was raped three times. For all those beasts knew, they raped a cadaver. God was not beside me as I lay upon those rocks." She leans in close and makes sure he is looking her in the eye. "For if He was, Elias—if He was truly there as you say—then *He* is the monster. For allowing this to happen to me, *your* God is the monster. And you are nothing but one of his demons." Anna lets go with a shriek of a laugh that startles even herself. "You are nothing more than an imp." Standing erect, she towers before him. "Now…Get. Out. And rest assured. I won't follow you again. Get out."

Elias gives one last look of pity, then one of repulsion, before turning to leave much faster than he arrived. He's in such a hurry that he does not notice Josef there, walking toward Anna. The clockmaker ignores the priestly blur skirting from his shop. His attention is upon his assistant, who is exposed to the world, standing before him.

"Anna?"

It isn't until the door closes and Elias is fully out of view that she hears her name. Even then, her voice is faraway. "Yes?"

"What's happened?" Josef asks, unsure of exactly what it is he should be asking. "Is everything…? Are you all right?"

Anna seems to awaken from a trance. With a gasp, she covers her chest with her arms. She stutters to explain, but no discernable words come out. Josef waves her silent and kneels to gather her dress. He drapes it over her shoulders and wraps her shaking body.

With a look of understanding and a tone of compassion that brings a tear to her eye, Josef says, "There's no need to explain, my dear. I heard enough."

He collects the rest of her garments and carries them from the room.

"Josef?" Anna says. "I need to go home. For a little while."

He nods. "I'll finish your new legs as soon as I can."

EIGHT

Of

ENDINGS AND BEGINNINGS

Josef outdoes himself in the construction of Anna's new legs. They have the basic mechanics of the first set but with a few improvements. For one, they have extended self-walking capabilities, with greater sensitivity, perpetuated by gentle the rhythm of her pelvis. Her gait becomes subtler; the swivel bearings that are now her hip joints make for a smoother, more natural stride. She continues to use her cane in the beginning, but it's not long before she gains enough confidence to rely upon it less.

Anna does not have to cringe at the sight of her legs now, for Josef has fitted them with leggings of wool and lambskin, woven for durability with strands of silver and gold—a kind of gilded flesh. The unique material not only creates a skin-like appearance, but a physical warmth to the touch. Most importantly, when Anna runs her hand down her legs—which she now does every morning before dressing—she feels whole, almost human.

The enhancements that bring Anna the greatest pleasure are the imperceptible levers that activate springs that, in accordance with slight adjustments of her weight, allow her to kneel, jump, and best of all, to ascend and descend steps. It takes practice to make these simple actions second nature. And practice she does.

For hours each the day, Josef hears the clumping of Anna upon the stairs. He watches her move about the shop and sees a joy in her the likes of which he's never seen before. She beams innocently at any opportunity to venture outside the shop and conquer the cobbled streets of Salzburg.

"To see her less unhappy is a little disconcerting," Josef confesses to Christoph. "All we know of her is misery, really."

"You know nothing of her life before Salzburg?"

"She grew up on a farm. That's all I know. She never mentioned the priest until he showed up here. Now I'm concerned about this desire she has to go home."

"She said she knows of a source for fine crystals,"

Christoph muses.

"Out there? On a farm?" Josef lowers his brow, skeptical. "She doesn't even know how long she'll be gone."

"She said a few days, remember?"

"A lot can happen in a few days. Springs could bind. Gears might seize. Hinges may lock."

"I'm sure you'll give her legs a thorough examination before she goes so none of those things happen." Christoph grins.

"Why are you smiling?"

"You're not concerned about her legs. You're worried she may not want to return to Salzburg."

"Of course," Josef replies. "Her assistance here has proven invaluable. She's spoiled me."

"Or perhaps you've come to see her as more than an assistant."

"Nonsense."

"Is it?"

Josef's reluctance to continue the conversation reveals his probable answer. Christoph lets the matter rest there.

As for Anna, she is not entirely sure why she is

going, either. Besides the crystals, she's being drawn homeward for some inexplicable reason, and it seems going home is the only way to discover what that reason is.

❂ ❧ ❂ ❧ ❂

Resigning to the fact that the only way Anna can make her journey is by carriage, Josef hires the best post chaise and driver he can find.

The road Anna first traveled to Salzburg is the same, but it feels different because she is different. Anna recalls a life dictated by seasons as she's taken past the communal fields. Her childhood memories are of the comfort of routine. Seeding, growing, and harvest, year in and year out. She rose early to accompany her father each morning, and her strong legs once managed the mudded pastures with ease when she returned to their house of wood and stone to help her mother.

Being the eldest, there were certain expectations of Anna, most of which were to care for her younger sister and brother, Nadette and Karl. They weren't so much younger than her that they didn't try Anna's patience and challenge her authority. She did not complain, however. Finding fault in others was not in her nature. She adored her siblings and never tired of them.

On the evenings she remembers most fondly, her father would take out his pochette and play by firelight. The flickering of the flames kept in lively rhythm with his vigorous bowing. He never played sad or brooding songs. Every tune was full of zest and worthy of a dance. Anna's preference, though, was to simply sit and listen.

By her request, the coachman, Freidrich, takes Anna a short distance beyond the farm fields to a wooded area where the road stops. Freidrich comes to her carriage door and makes it known that he is wary of the secluded location before opening it. (Josef paid him extra to also act as chaperon.) Anna assures him that she will be fine and points to a narrow trail that leads to a house of wood and sod visible from the road.

"I shouldn't be long," Anna tells him, "and I'll be no farther than there."

Neither the house nor the woods appear particularly foreboding, yet the coachman still nods with obvious apprehension. For a moment, Anna questions the decision to leave her cane in Salzburg. She takes a deep breath and gratefully accepts Freidrich's hand as he assists her in stepping down from the carriage.

Another breath. She moves a few steps. Then a few more. She holds back a giddy tear as she walks the path into the woods with ease. The trail which she has traversed before is no longer familiar. Underbrush has grown in and over it, making the path even more crooked and narrow. Anna feels like a stranger. She imagines the woman who lives there to impart familiarity.

Vadoma Wiel.

She recalls the reddish-brown hue of her skin. That the Wiels came from southern lands was all she knew of their heritage. Vadoma's husband, the wheelmaker, died before Anna was born. The couple never had children. And so, to Anna's recollection, Frau Wiel was always the old woman who lived alone in the house behind the trees. Some locals called her a gypsy. Some a witch. Others called her a sorceress for her unique skills in healing, fortunes, and spells. One season, when other communities were experiencing an unexpected blight, the farms around Anna prospered. Those families attributed their good fortune to

Vadoma's magic. Now, however, Anna isn't here for her alleged magic, but the woman's beautiful crystals.

Anna raps on the house's thin, warped door. It's going on three years now that Anna has been away; she can't recall the last time she saw the old woman. When there is no answer, she wonders if she is even still alive. Anna knocks again, much harder, then fears the door will come off its hinges.

A voice comes from within. "Who's there? Who is calling?"

Anna is surprised by the voice's clear, vibrant tone. There's no sign of frailty in it. She replies, "I am Annamarie Klor. I'm looking for Frau Wiel."

The door creaks open and reveals Vadoma. She is just as Anna remembers her.

"I am here, Fräulein Klor," Vadoma says with a yellow-toothed grin. She opens the door wider. "What a joy to see you again. Please, come in. How you've grown, dear."

Anna ducks to enter the two-room house. Its interior is warmed by the glow of a fire that dutifully keeps the chill of the coming fall at bay. The air is thick with sage, tea, and the mustiness from closed windows.

The walls are so lined with shelves of books, dishes, figurines, and bottles that one might wonder if there are indeed walls behind them. By all appearances, it is the shelves that hold up the home's ragged roof. Anna finds a small space to stand within the clutter of furniture and turns to her host.

"You look very well, Frau Wiel."

Vadoma looks her guest over, then grimaces. "My dear, what has happened to your head? Your eye?"

Anna often forgets her cockeyed appearance. She turns away shyly. "The result of a bad fall."

"I'm sorry?" Vadoma leans in.

"I fell down," Anna says louder.

"Oh, my. From quite a height, I imagine. Or were you pushed?" When Anna becomes visibly uncomfortable, Vadoma adds, "But it is such flaws that bring out the beauty within, my dear. Look at me. A greater vision of flawed splendor you will not find."

Anna smiles.

"Now, what is the reason for this visit?"

"I am looking for a pair of crystals."

Vadoma's brow furrows. "Did you say crystals?"

Anna increases her volume. "Yes, crystals. I

recall you always had the finest."

"For what purpose? What are your intentions? Do you need inspiration or something to balance your mood? Or is it peace you're looking for? It's not love, is it? What of the young man you went to Salzburg to marry?"

Her thoughts spin from the old woman's questions. Anna takes a moment. "No, it's nothing like that. For aesthetic reasons only. I just need something to give off a sparkle of light."

"Something to spark life?"

"No. *Light*. Something that will catch the light and shine."

Vadoma steps back. She takes in the sight of her guest once more and inhales as though breathing in Anna's presence. The old woman smiles. "My dear, the light of life is so very strong within you. I remember how it always emanated from you. It still does, more than ever. Whatever would you need the power of crystals for?"

"They are not for me. They are for a pair of eyes."

"Oh, the fall affected your vision."

"No. I can see fine." Anna leans forward and

speaks with the greatest clarity. "The crystals are to make a pair of eyes for a figurine. A doll."

"You want to bring a doll to life?"

"Well, so to speak," Anna tries to explain. "The *illusion* of life, you might say. Reflection from the right stones could certainly do that, couldn't they?"

Frau Wiel grins, and offers Anna a knowing nod, and then crosses the room to a bureau of what must be a hundred small drawers. Anna thinks little of the old woman mumbling something about the difficulty of animating the inanimate. Instead, she watches with nostalgic delight as Vadoma rummages through drawer after drawer. When she returns, Frau Wiel holds out a pair of stones. Anna takes one, turns it to the firelight, and lets out a gentle gasp at how it flickers brilliant blues, greens, and yellows. They take in the light and reflect it back tenfold.

"Rainbow Moonstone," Vadoma tells her. "It glows of the sun *and* the moon. It is a stone of transformation."

"It's so…" But Anna can find no words to convey its beauty. "It's perfect."

"And *imperfect*, if you look closely. Like yourself,

Annamarie, its loveliness is within its flaws."

Anna hands the stone back. "Thank you, Frau Wiel. I'll take them."

"Give me until tomorrow to properly prepare them."

"Prepare?"

"To cleanse and purify them," Vadoma explains. "Then you'll want to hold them and keep them close to you at all times. Let them absorb the power of your inner light. The longer you can put your thoughts on their purpose, the greater effect their enchantment will have, and the greater *life* the stones will give."

"The better they will reflect *light*, you mean."

Vadoma nods with a grin.

A little off balance from the fire's heat, Anna says, "Tomorrow, then?"

"Yes. Tomorrow."

Freidrich finds Anna an inn for the night. She still plans to visit her family; she is simply not ready yet. That night, Anna finds it hard to sleep, troubled by memories of the last time she saw her parents, her brother, and sister, and the lie she told them to make leaving easier. To this day, the Klors believe their daughter went to Salzburg to marry the love of her youth. "Because," as she so eloquently fabricated, "he's decided not to be a priest. He has chosen me over the Church and has asked me to join him posthaste."

There were protests and lamentations about the lack of a proper wedding, of course, but Anna explained that Elias had already established an apprenticeship he couldn't leave and a house he couldn't manage alone. He had, according to Anna, found them a new life. All that was missing was her.

Elias's parents believed this as well, having heard it from the Klors. The blissfully naïve Dorns never questioned how Elias failed to mention his new life and marriage in his letters from the seminary. The Dorns have passed on in the time since, and so Anna is allowed to maintain her deceit. Now she looks to her return home with lingering dread, knowing she will have to perpetuate the lie she began years before and concoct new ones.

At first, Anna is on the outside looking in. She spots the humble house where she grew up, much more cared for than Frau Wiel's, and she glides along the community pastures that line the road. She hears the bray of goats and the low-pitched clucks of hens warning their chicks to stay close as Anna nears. She senses a busyness in the air as harvest approaches and takes in the unmistakable smell of damp earth. Stepping from the carriage and landing on her feet, Anna finds herself within what seems to be the ending (yet at the same time, the beginning) to a bitter-sweet fairy tale. Her family wraps her in their arms. There are tears of joy and laughter tinged with sorrow. There are the questions, lots of questions:

What is Salzburg like?

"Beautiful and crowded."

How is Elias?

"He is well."

What does he do?

"He's…a clockmaker."

We worried when your letters stopped coming.

"Yes, I'm sorry. I'll do better."

What happened to your face?

"I took a bad fall."

Are those really the clothes of a clockmaker's wife? So

refined.

"Not as refined as you might think."

Can I ride in the carriage?

"Perhaps later, Karl."

Will there be children soon? It's not too late.

"God willing."

The lies she tells come easy because they are sown with truths. Except for the last one—God willing or not, it is too late. The demon count had beat the ability to have children out of her as well as crippled her. Otherwise, the lies are like the one she told when she left the first time. She *did* go away to marry the love of her youth. At least, that was her intention.

Anna sits with her family and hears of their lives, which have not changed, not even a little. As they speak, she considers her own past here at the farm.

What future did it offer besides monotonous days and tea?

Hot chocolate was unknown to her then. Anna longs for a cup of it now.

Did I truly love Elias, or was he just an excuse to leave?

No. She did love him. He was more than a distraction from the ordinary. And she loved her family as well. She *loves* her family. But Anna always had a penchant for the unconventional; she never thought of herself as one to follow tradition: marry, have children, and then more children. In Salzburg—with Josef, especially—there has been nothing conventional. She still has the comfort of her routines, but they are much more unique now. Certainly, she wishes the circumstances of meeting the clockmaker had been different. Nonetheless...

It is at that moment Anna realizes why she came home.

To say goodbye.

Lives change like the seasons, and this, too, is Anna's harvesttime. The farm is no longer her home. It is in Salzburg.

A strange, melancholic peace falls over her. She enjoys a meal of potatoes, bread, and for this special occasion, lamb. She gives her family the gift of a small clock she brought along. It is a modest piece. At the same time, it is the most resplendent thing they have ever seen. She spies her father's pochette in a corner by the hearth and asks him to play a tune. He gladly bows a familiar melody, the name of which Anna cannot recall.

She gives Karl and Nadette a ride in the carriage before leaving. In her coat pocket, she holds with her left hand the moonstone crystals she acquired from Frau Wiel earlier that morning. As she observes the glee on her sibling's faces, Anna feels the sensation of her fingers warming the stones. During her ride back to Salzburg, however, she wonders if the strange sensation might actually be the stones themselves warming her fingers.

NINE

Of

TIME'S BIDDING

It has been a while since Josef tended his shop alone. As instructed by Anna, he begins the day with time spent in company of the menagerie. The critters are wary of his presence at first, but they soon recognize him and agitate with excitement.

"Yes, my old friends," he says, "it is good to see you, too. It hasn't been that long, has it?"

Galileo head-butts Josef's hand with enough force to knock a food dish from it. Ramses the rat hurries to the clockmaker and puts its front feet upon his arm. If not for his wheeled back end, the brown rodent would certainly climb up to Josef's shoulder. He laughs as Ramses frantically sniffs the fibers of his jacket. Sneaky the squirrel keeps his distance upon a shelf but click-click-clicks away like an overwound clock. The raven, resting on a perch near Josef's head, let's out the most startling of caws.

"Oh, Annabel, you beautiful thing." The clockmaker extends an arm for her to hop to. "Yes, I owe you a set of wings, don't I? I promise to give them my utmost attention." Josef looks around at the room of rescues as they chirp, purr, and sniff. "This visit is long overdue, isn't it? Even after Anna's return, I'll make sure to spend more time here."

If she returns.

Like all his rescues—his experiments—Josef never thought about what he would do with Anna. He only knew that she needed help. He didn't consider what might become of her afterward. Frankly, he's ashamed to recall that he hadn't thought she would live. Yet, she did.

It wasn't his idea to have an assistant. That was a responsibility she took upon herself. Even before being fully recovered and mastering her mobility, Anna took to cleaning and organizing the backroom. She then made her way through the rest of the shop. It wasn't long before the broken woman proved herself a valuable addition to the clockmaker's life—especially when she began making hot chocolate for him.

In her absence, it will prove the most frustrating part of Josef's day, for he knows he won't get the concoction quite right. His fault will lie in allowing the chocolate to boil after adding the egg yolk, thus curdling it. After a few failed attempts, he'll give up. He will, however, make an acceptable effort at maintaining the shop to the standards Anna has set.

He will also feel her presence clinging like the aroma of roses and edelweiss and find himself thinking of her at every turn. The image of her standing naked in the shop—a strangely arousing vision of steel and flesh—will creep into his thoughts at odd occasions. Fortunately, he'll have plenty to distract him. The list of chores she made. Appointments with clients.

None of that before a visit with Joop, though.

"Now, my boy, what would you like to do today? Walk? Dance a bit? Hear a story?" Josef waits, then laughs at himself for expecting a response. "How about a game of hide-and-seek?"

He takes a disc from the box and inserts it into the mechanized child. Joop pops into action with a turn toward Joseph, then he runs to hide around the corner of a worktable.

Josef pretends to search the area. "Now, where did that boy go?"

The clockmaker steps a little closer, and Joop scoots backwards into a shadow. Josef makes a deliberate turn away, putting his back to the boy. He waits for Joop to sneak up and grab his leg. Josef spins around in surprise. The clockwork lad jumps in a replication of joy and claps his hands together. The clockmaker kneels down, and they hug. For a minute after Joop has resumed an inanimate state, Josef continues to hug him.

Later that first morning without Anna, the clockmaker has an appointment with Stefan Peiper, the Marquis de Castile. Monsieur Peiper stands before the clockmaker with greater agitation than he had during their first meeting; the telling of his unusual circumstances was nothing compared to the anticipation of actually seeing his peculiar request come to fruition.

"I think you'll be pleased with this," Josef tells the marquis. The clockmaker removes the lid from a box and folds back the protective velvet cloth.

Stefan's eyes widen in a way that leaves Josef wondering: is it a look of immense joy, or disheartened shock? The phallus of polished steel rests in the box like a fine weapon waiting to be taken in hand for a duel. Stefan hesitates before taking it. "It is not as heavy as it appears."

"That is because it is hollow," Josef explains. "There's a reservoir within which you can add hot water, thus warming the outer surface to better replicate your own body temperature."

Stefan grows comfortable with the object and explores it with his other hand. "What of this ribbed texture?"

"For her pleasure."

Josef reveals a small key in his palm, inserts it into the base, and gives it a few turns. The gentle vibration of the penis tickles the marquis's fingers. At the object's base, there is a coupled bearing connecting it to the body of the phallus. Stefan takes the base firmly in one hand and moves the steel shaft in a circular motion with the other.

"That swivel allows it to move with her as she moves," Josef tells him.

Stefan searches for something to say and manages simply, "Remarkable."

Josef sighs in relief. "You find it satisfactory?"

"I never could have imagined."

"But you did imagine. Now here it is." From another box, Josef removes a leather corset with adjustable straps. "You can fit this around your groin. The penis will fasten here"—he demonstrates—"allowing you to use it as though it were your own."

Stefan places the mechanical phallus back into its box with exaggerated reverence, relieving the previous moment's tension.

"I fear of being crude," Josef says, "but I'll be interested to know how this works for the two of you."

The marquis laughs. He takes Josef's hand in a grateful, lingering grasp, then leaves without a word more.

A short time later, while immersed in designing improvements to Count Meusberger's legs, Josef senses someone in the shop. He comes a cordial yet authoritative voice. "Good morning. Is anyone here?"

If Anna has taught the clockmaker anything, it is the importance of customers to his livelihood. This awareness helps him tolerate the annoyance of interruptions. He takes a deep breath and ventures from his study.

Bishop von Bohn stands among the displays, at once pleased and disappointed about being greeted by Josef. "I was hoping to speak with your assistant. Annamarie, isn't it?"

"Yes. She is not here at the moment. I don't expect her back for a few days."

"Everything is all right with her, I hope."

"Of course. She needed a little time away."

"Don't we all," von Bohn replies.

Josef moves to lead the bishop toward the door. "I'll let her know you stopped by."

His Excellency keeps his place. "But I'm thinking now, perhaps you're the one I should be talking to."

"Oh?"

"She's a rare woman, Annamarie is."

Josef hesitates before agreeing. "Yes, she is."

"It seems there's much more to her than first appears."

Now Josef understands. "I take it this is about her legs. You heard something from the priest. Dorn? He has told you of a recent event here in my shop."

"Is it true?"

"Yes. Apparently, he and Anna have a history."

"No, no." The bishop looks at Josef with an inquisitive grin, his brows raised. "Her legs? Her hand?" He raises his own for emphasis.

"When I met Anna, she was severely…incapacitated. Nearly dead. To save her life, her hand and legs were removed. Once we knew she would survive, I equipped her with new appendages of steel and springs. She has managed well enough, as you've seen."

The bishop's eyes beam. "I would say she has managed quite well."

Josef gives him a questioning look.

"I apologize for my impetuous intrusion," the bishop explains, "but I have a penchant for mechanics and engineering. A personal fascination, you might say. A *passion*, really, I must confess. At times, I regret…" The bishop stops himself with a shake of his head.

Josef smiles. "A true confession, it seems. I'm sorry I do not have an oratory within which His Excellency could kneel."

The bishop laughs. "Truth be told, then, I'd very much like to talk with you about your work sometime. The perpetual clock. These appendages. Are there others?"

"*Sometime* it will have to be." Josef raises a calming hand to slow the enthusiastic bishop. "At the moment, I must get back my work. When Anna returns, we'll have you join us for dinner." The clockmaker, again, starts for the front door. This time, the bishop follows.

"Yes, yes. That sounds lovely. I am sorry to have bothered you."

"No bother at all, Your Excellency. An enlightening surprise, actually. One that I will enjoy indulging another time."

With a respectful bow, Josef bids the bishop a good day.

When Dr. Baeder stops in for a game of backgammon, Josef shares about his encounter with Bishop von Bohn.

"Oh?" is Christoph's initial response. Then he falls quiet.

"His Excellency was quite giddy. I find his excitement over my work charming."

"I would think *unexpected* to be a better word."

"You find his knowledge of Anna worrisome?"

Christoph answers only with a weighted shrug.

"I can't imagine the Church would care one way or another about what we've done. Consider Friar Albert of Cologne. It's said he had great interest in natural science and was a bit of an alchemist. He's attributed with constructing a mechanical head of brass that could speak and answer any question put to it. An oracle of sorts."

"Yes, I've heard that tale," Christoph says. "I've also heard that his student Thomas Aquinas took a hammer to it for talking too much."

They laugh.

"It is not the Church I find suspect, but fools who act on its behalf."

"Bishop von Bohn is no fool."

"No, but he is a Brunner. And what of this priest?" He rolls of the dice. "I wonder sometimes if Anna wasn't wrong in her thinking. That letting her remain legless, or Pascal without a hand, wouldn't have been a better choice. More dignified."

"Yes, dragging oneself across the floor reeks of dignity."

"What of a wheeled chair? We use them at the hospital."

"For the infirmed and powerless, perhaps. Neither of which is Anna. Besides, they have their limitations and are no more dignified, in my mind."

"Doesn't dignity come from how we respond to adversity? Besides the immediate benefits, are we really doing anyone any good in the greater scheme of things?"

Josef sighs with the heaviest of breath.

They finish their game and start another. Eventually Christoph says, "I'm impressed with how well you've recovered. But I have to say, this heart should be your last."

"Three are enough for any man, I suppose," agrees Josef.

The two friends then spend the rest of the game in silence.

The next day, a messenger arrives at the shop early. The note comes from Duke Leopold Brunner, who requests the presence of the clockmaker at the earliest possible time.

Josef has reservations regarding the invitation. For one, it is Leopold Brunner, a man who is not high on his favorable list. Another is the fact that his wife is a woman Josef prefers not to be distracted by any longer. Yet the exigency of the request is intriguing, and Josef does have a weakness for intrigue.

Inside the Brunner palace, the clockmaker is led through the foyer to the sitting room. His uncomfortable desire to see Klara is at odds with his need to forget her. Disappointment and relief collide when he finds four gentlemen awaiting his arrival.

Duke Brunner sits royally but tired in an Italian armchair. Standing to his right is Herr Weisman, whose beady eyes take in Josef with the same wariness one would expect of a jittery canine. To the right of Weisman is Bishop von Bohn. Josef glimpses in his eyes the spirited gleam of their encounter the day before. And, unexpectedly, on Leopold Brunner's left stands Christoph.

Josef shares a look with the doctor. "This summons becomes more interesting by the moment."

"Thank you for coming so promptly, Herr Kronecker," the duke says. "You've met Herr Weisman, I believe. Do you know my brother, the bishop? Of course you do. Naturally, you know Herr Doctor, whom I've taken on as my physician."

"Yes, Duke, sir." After a cordial exchange of bows with the others, Josef says, "I came as soon as I could, having sensed a certain urgency in your message. Though, I can't imagine what such immediate concerns my skills could possibly address."

"A humble man you are," replies the duke. "The matter concerns my health, Herr Kronecker—Josef, if I may. More specifically, the problem, you see, is with my heart…"

As the duke speaks, Josef looks again to Christoph. His friend gives an apologetic shrug and a wordless plea of open hands. Josef then becomes aware of the duke telling him, "There's no need to worry. Your secret is safe. It will not leave this room."

"A trite matter now, really," replies Josef.

"Exactly. I much rather you'd consider my request."

"You'd like me to make you a heart."

"Yes."

"Time is of the essence."

Brunner nods, then adds with a softened tone, "Just when I had come to terms with the brief time I have left in this world, I find that it may not have to be so brief after all. I had given up hope, but perhaps now I *could* accomplish that which has eluded me for so long. As you may know, I cannot father children. But with the finest doctor in Salzburg—or anywhere—now in my employ and the possibility of more time…well, you can imagine my renewed optimism.”

“Time. An endless resource of which there never seems to be enough,” Josef says. “You do realize this decision could alternately expediate your demise?”

The duke turns to Christoph, urging him to contribute to his argument.

Reluctantly, the doctor acquiesces. “I have warned the duke of the risks and that there are no certainties. Like yourself, Josef, Leopold is in otherwise fine enough physical condition. A good candidate for the procedure. He simply needs a new heart.”

“It is a gamble I’m willing to take,” Brunner adds. “The sooner the better.”

“There is no ‘simply’ about it,” Josef says. “And ‘sooner’ may not be soon enough. You must know that even if I expediate the process, it could take months.”

“That is why I hope you will begin work this very

day. Let me add, Josef, you can expect to be very well compensated."

Herr Weisman finally speaks, his voice a sharp bark cutting the air. "Perhaps…"

The men turn to him.

"…you could *simply* give Duke Brunner *your* heart." His smile is unmistakably antagonistic.

Brunner emits a humorless laugh. Christoph furrows his brow.

The bishop speaks up. "To answer your question at the start, Josef—you do possess the skills my brother urgently needs. You're the only man in the world that does. His life is in your hands."

Josef turns from the men to contemplate his options. He could refuse, knowing Leopold Brunner is a man who does not take refusal lightly. It is one thing to replace another's hand or legs; if he's not successful, the subject still lives. But, as the bishop stated, he would be responsible for the duke's life—a loathsome life, in Josef's opinion, but a life nonetheless.

He could accept, and if he did, he would do, as always, his finest work. The rest would be up to fate. In the months it would take to construct the device, there would be the possibility of the duke's own heart failing, meaning he would die naturally. There's also a chance the bastard might not survive the surgery. On the other hand, it could go so well that the duke could thrive for many years to come. *Would that be so horrible*, Christoph might observe, *in the greater scheme of things?*

There is also the matter of a generous compensation.

"Dr. Baeder, I will need all you have regarding the duke's present physical state." Josef turns to the duke. "I will begin designing a heart for you as soon as I return to my studio."

A genuine, heartfelt laugh bursts from Leopold.

The bishop, too, is elated, though his elation is subtler.

Herr Weisman gives a not-so-genuine grin.

Christoph does not smile, or say anything.

⊕   ⧉   ⊕   ⧉   ⊕

Herr Weisman finds the duchess reclining upon her favorite French chaise lounge reading a recently acquired copy of *Memoirs of a Woman of Pleasure*. She makes him wait until she reaches a satisfactory place to pause before looking up.

"Yes?" At the sight of the confidant's shrewd smirk, she sits up straight. "What is it?"

"You may want to buy some new dresses," Weisman tells her. "Distracting, provocative dresses."

Josef begins his third day without Anna tending the menagerie, staying only long enough to feed and water them before getting back to the work he'd begun on Duke Brunner's heart. He worked through the night sans sleep—the first time since his recovery.

Fortunately for the duke, Josef already has the most tedious part of the process completed. All he has to do is make appropriate modifications in his original plans to accommodate Leopold's larger size. What took Josef nine months for his cardio mechanism should take a mere three for the duke's—as long as interruptions are kept to a minimum, that is. Which, without Anna, proves difficult.

The first is a browsing customer. Josef's impatience gets the best of him when he realizes the gentleman is only there to look and not buy, and he ushers the man out of the shop like a cold wind.

Then there's the flower girl with a bouquet of purple gentian and the news of the morning. But the clockmaker has no interest in the petty lives of others this day. He takes the flowers and shoos the waif away.

Josef even has difficulty welcoming a visit from Pascal, who has come looking for Anna.

"She is not here," he tells the pianist. "She has gone home for a time."

"Oh, yes." Pascal frowns. "I'd forgotten."

"I wish I could say when she will return, but even she wasn't sure."

Pascal fidgets and lingers. He glances toward the front door a few times with the fleeting hope Anna will walk in.

"You're welcome to stay," Josef tells him. "Make yourself at home. Play a piece or two."

"I've practiced enough today. My fingers need a rest." A pause, then, "Is there something I could do to be of use to you?"

"Can you make hot chocolate?"

"I'm afraid not."

"Pity."

Josef has another idea and steps into his study. He returns with a piece of paper. On it, there's a list. "Normally, I would have Anna do this. Perhaps, in her absence, you could…?"

"Yes. Of course."

"These are parts I need for a project. Could you check to see what I have in my inventory and note what I will need to request from the metal forger? Anna keeps the bins well categorized and labeled."

Pascal smiles. "I imagine she does."

Josef laughs. "Misplace anything and she will see that I have to make you another appendage of some kind."

Pascal makes his way to the backroom. Josef was right. Anna has everything in its place, labeled and arranged just so, like a great clockwork library. The young man is so impressed that his adoration of her fills his heart like never before. Silly, really, for such a thing as neatness to have that effect. As though he needed anything more to clarify his emotions for this peculiar, aloof woman. Yet, there it is, making him ache with immeasurable longing while he stands alone in a space she commonly occupies. He curses his youth, which he's convinced is the single obstacle to keeping him from being with her. If both of them having only one hand can't spark a romantic bond between them, then what else could?

The sound of a small footfall upon the floor comes from a dark corner of the room. Pascal turns and squints, peering into the darkness. A faint meow pierces the shadow.

"You must be the Galileo I've heard so much about," Pascal says. "So, we finally meet." He kneels and puts out his hand in greeting.

The feline emerges. The steel appendages that make up his hind quarters give the pianist a start. Galileo approaches with a hopping gait. Pascal's surprise quickly turns into fascination. He runs his fingers over the cat's arching back and touches the mechanical device that propels the animal forward.

Pascal watches with great interest as Galileo meows and purrs and circles the space. There's an aspect of the cat's gait which the pianist finds familiar but can't quite place. Then, in a manner only part-mechanical felines and peculiar, aloof women apparently do, Galileo turns from Pascal with a curt twitch of his tail and dismissive meow before hopping away.

The truth about Anna comes to Pascal like a crescendo.

As soon as it hits him, the thought is disrupted by someone entering the shop. Pascal heads from the backroom to find Duchess Brunner amongst the displays, seeming reticent to enter farther. She gives a pleased if not slightly puzzled smile at the sight of the pianist.

"Herr Künzi, what a lovely surprise."

"How nice it is to see you, Duchess. I am assisting Herr Kronecker in Anna's absence."

"Oh, yes. Josef has been left to himself, hasn't he?" Klara says brightly. Then, more to herself, "All the better."

"Is there something I can assist you with?" Pascal asks.

"You're a dear, but I imagine I will find him in his study?"

"If you'll wait, I'll see if——"

"I am here," says Josef, appearing from behind a row of clocks. "Thank you, Pascal."

"Josef." Klara tilts her head in greeting.

The clockmaker notices a look he has never seen from the duchess before—one he finds difficult to label. Apprehension? Bewilderment? Fear?

"Might we speak in private?" she asks.

Josef gestures for her to follow him to the study.

The duchess walks with her usual composure, but as soon as Josef closes the door behind them, her poise drops to the floor like heavy armor and she throws her arms around him, nestling her head into his shoulder. Taken aback, Josef returns the embrace without hesitation. He welcomes it, even. They hold each other until their breathing synchronizes.

"Thank you, Josef. Thank you."

He closes his eyes and relishes her breath against his neck. "For what?"

"For my husband's heart."

Feeling him recoil, Klara leans back just enough to look into his eyes. "Please, appreciate the position I'm in. Leopold has given so much to me. I may not have married him for love, but I've never wished him ill." She presses a hand to his face. "Now, to have the man I truly adore come to his aid leaves me…"

Josef takes her hand. With a tender but hesitant

grip, he moves it from his cheek to his chest. Emotions he once thought subdued now resurge and send him into a vertiginous plummet. "I'm conflicted as well," he tells her. "What am I to do?"

"What are *we* to do?"

Josef takes in the question with a heavy sigh. "We are at time's bidding. All we can do is wait and work."

She gives the hand that holds hers a long, tender kiss. Then she moves her mouth toward his. A voice comes from the shop. Josef turns his head before their lips can meet. "Christoph?"

The doctor enters. If he is surprised at the sight of his friend and the duchess awkwardly parting from their embrace, he does not show it. Instead, Christoph smiles and bows. "How nice to see you, Duchess Brunner."

Her mouth turns downward, and she puts her hand out to him. "I much preferred it when you called me Klara."

Christoph takes her hand.

Klara looks to Josef. "I should be going."

"Yes. Of course," he replies.

The two share a lingering gaze. The gentle swish

of her dress across the Aubusson rug punctuates her departure. Josef and Christoph are left alone with a silence as uncomfortable as a funeral between them.

Christoph breaks it. "You couldn't wait until he's dead?"

"As a matter of fact, we are." Josef smirks.

Christoph's eyebrows raise.

Josef turns away from his friend's glare. "What was I to do, Christoph? I wanted to refuse Brunner's request. But honestly, how could I?" His shoulders droop. "No matter the choice, my motives would have been suspect."

"They weren't," Christoph says, "until a moment ago."

His back to the doctor, Josef leans against his worktable, his head hanging over the drawings for Leopold Brunner's new heart. "Am I just a foolish old man?"

"Yes."

Josef chuckles.

"You are a man who has somehow captured the attention of a woman of rare qualities. You are allowed a modicum of foolishness."

The clockmaker looks in the direction of Klara's departure. "Something has always seemed so familiar about her," he says dreamily. "It makes her presence strangely comfortable."

Christoph steps forward and puts a hand on his friend's shoulder. "As your doctor and friend, I would advise you to tread carefully."

Josef straightens his posture with newfound determination. "What I need to do is finish this damnable device and be done with the whole blessed mess."

"Spoken like the stalwart old fool I know."

After a laugh, Josef asks, "Besides interrupting my tryst with a duchess, what is the reason for your visit this morning?"

"To apologize," Christoph explains. "I'm sorry, Josef, that I did not warn you of the duke's interest in your work."

"I thought something was on your mind the other day besides backgammon."

"He's been highly outspoken of late on the subject of immortality with anyone who will lend him an ear."

"Immortality? Only an idiot would want to live

forever."

"I should have expected where it would lead. But I didn't foresee this request for a new heart."

"Oh, so now you are a seer of the future?"

"No, but logic dictates outcome."

"There's no logic with madmen."

Before Christoph can respond, Josef abruptly leaves the study, mumbling something about Pascal and a list. Christoph follows with curiosity.

In the shop, Josef stops suddenly, as does Christoph, just before colliding into the clockmaker. Before them stands a most beguiling woman. Her allure lies not in the bulky folds of her basquine or in the delicate lace of her mantilla as it falls from her shoulders and collects conservatively across her chest. Her attraction is in her dark, burning eyes. Eyes that Christoph recognizes just as Josef speaks.

"Marquess Pieper. How may I assist you?"

With the coyest of expressions, the marquess steps toward the clockmaker. She extends her hand, which Josef takes. She then covers his with her other hand and wraps it in a warm embrace. She leans in and kisses his right cheek, then his left, lingering with such tender gratitude that Christoph feels he must graciously look away. The marquess leans back and mouths the words, "*Thank—you—*" before leaving the shop as quietly as she arrived.

In the church-like lull that follows the clack of the closing door, Christoph says, "You must one day share with me your peculiar secret with women."

TEN

Of

CRYSTAL EYES AGAIN...

Late on her third day away, Anna returns to the shop to little fanfare. She finds Josef in his study, of course, deeply occupied with his latest project. She lingers quietly, hesitant to interrupt, but soon the sense of voyeurism becomes too much.

"Hello?"

Josef looks up and as he turns, says, "Kla—" but stops at the sight of his assistant. "Anna, when did you—?"

"Just now. I don't mean to disturb you. I just wanted to let you know I am back."

"No, no, of course. Tell me, how was your trip?"

"It was lovely." Her fingers grip the moonstones in her pocket, which she has decided to surprise him with later. "Is there anything I can do for you before I retire?"

"Well," Josef gives her a crooked grin, "if you wouldn't mind?"

Anna smiles. "I'll bring you a cup momentarily."

She lights more candles in the study before leaving him to his work, then lights more throughout the shop and in the backroom. She finds a few bins out on a worktable that have been gone through. Clock parts are strewn about. It is apparent the menagerie has not been tended to, and she hopes the neglect has only been recent. For now, she sets to preparing a cup of hot chocolate.

In Josef's study, she places the warm cup within his reach. He gives a giddy chuckle and wraps both hands around it. "It is good to have you back," he tells her. "I do want to hear all about your trip in the morning."

"Of course. In the morning."

He stops her just before she leaves. "And your legs?"

"They worked without a flaw," she says. "Thank you."

Josef takes a long sip of chocolate.

Anna starts a fire in the hearth of her room. Foregoing candles, she uses the radiance from the fireplace to undress and dismantle her legs and hand. As is her preference, she lies back without a nightdress to feel the cool, comforting touch of the linens upon her skin. She looks about the space shrouded in yellow-orange warmth. How good it is to be home.

⚫ ❧ ⚫ ❧ ⚫

Anna and Josef say little to each other the following morning. His attention is so consumed by his work that she decides to address the issue of the moonstones on her own. She will deliver them to the gem-cutter with the required specifications needed to create Joop's eyes. Having had enough riding in a carriage to last her a while, Anna chooses to walk to her destination.

Her business with the gem-cutter requires little time. A need to be among others tugs at Anna, the desire to exchange cordial nods and "good mornings." Anything to feel common, accepted, and not a monster. She decides to take a meandering, aimless stroll homeward. She ventures into shops—in particular, a purveyor of fine timepieces. *Nothing but fine junk,* she concludes before moving on to a nearby chocolatier, where she can't resist the extravagant purchase of an apricot jam-filled Sacher torte. Lastly, before returning to home, Anna pays the flower girl a visit.

"I thought I might save you a trip to the shop today," she tells the waif.

"Yes, ma'am. It is good to see you. You seem well."

"I am, thank you. Quite well, actually."

"I have some dried heather, if you like."

"No." Anna purses her lips in thought. "I'd prefer a dash of color. Before the days become too dreary."

The girl directs her attention to a bouquet of trumpet gentian. Anna's eyes widen at their indigo hue. "How lovely." As she pays the girl, she asks, "Any news today?"

The girl takes a moment to think. "They say the duke has taken ill again."

Anna knows who "they" are without asking. She recalls during her initial period of servitude in Salzburg the grapevine of communique between the household menials, how far it reached, and how little the facts could be trusted. Yet, sometimes they could be.

"Oh? I hope he's faring well," Anna replies.

"For now, it seems. There were concerns. Not

that you would know by the duchess traipsing from one lover to another. But then, that is their arrangement.”

“Arrangement?”

“Because he cannot sire children, he allows her her pleasures in compensation.”

“I see.”

The girl leans close to Anna. “I’ve heard some say it is *she* who cannot have children and that she seduces physicians and the like into making the duke believe otherwise to keep her head. Can you imagine what it must take to carry out such a lie?”

“I cannot.”

“My father thinks both are true. That she is a lover *and* a liar. He worries sometimes what it would be like to be ruled by such a woman.”

Anna tips the girl, who pockets the money with humble gratitude. “Good day, Fräulein.”

Upon her return to the shop, Anna enters to the sound of laughter. If she didn’t know better, she would guess it was the merriment of children. Stopping to listen, however, she discerns it is Josef and a woman. The chortles emanate from the backroom. She sets down the cake and wild flowers, and makes her way in that direction. Not too fast, but certainly not slow. She pulls back the curtain. She sees no one, but the voices are louder. Her stomach tightens at the light coming through the open door to the menagerie. Without hesitation, she moves toward it.

The sight Anna beholds freezes her: Josef and Klara standing with the collection of misfit critters that scurry, squeak, and squawk about them. Klara's hand is upon Josef's shoulder in a more than cordial manner. She clutches him tenderly as she laughs.

"Oh, Josef. This is absolutely marvelous."

The duchess is the first to notice that she and Josef are no longer alone.

"Annamarie," she says with relaxed familiarity. "Look. I was right. You do have rats."

Josef turns with merely a glance at Anna before looking, back to Klara. "And squirrels."

The two of them laugh.

Anna backs away from the room—not an easy feat, even with her new legs, but she finds she must move away from Josef and the duchess, even as she's unable to take her eyes from the scene before her. Lost in a flirtatious daze, they hardly notice her departure.

Over the days that follow, Anna's consternation grows along with Klara's presence in the shop. Two, sometimes three times a day, the duchess stops in for a visit. Anna is subjected to the couple's stomach-churning ogling and persistent laughter. She wonders how Josef could possibly be getting any work done. When the clockmaker calls for assistance, it is usually for another cup of chocolate or a tea for the duchess. Klara is so courteous with Anna that she finds it difficult to nurture obstinance toward the woman. Yet, as soon as she leaves the two lovers alone, Anna's torturous imaginings return. *Lovers?* she wonders with grave and nauseating uncertainty.

A week passes, and the one thing Anna most dreaded comes to fruition: Josef invites Klara to stay for dinner. The fact that Anna serves boiled-beef and potatoes does not escape Josef.

"This is what you've come up with?" he asks as the three of them sit to dine.

"I wasn't expecting a guest today," Anna replies. "Otherwise, I would've been better prepared."

"I see," he says.

Klara peruses the meal with a discerning gaze,

then straightens in her chair and smiles. "This is lovely, Annamarie. Thank you."

Josef gives the duchess a sideways glance.

"It *is* lovely. This food reminds me of my childhood." Turning to Anna, she adds, "I came from a humble home, like you. My family farmed south of here."

"Now here you are," says Anna. "A duchess."

Klara laughs. "True. By circumstances one typically finds only in children's tales."

They each enjoy a bite from their plate. Klara gives a satisfied hum, then resumes her exchange with Anna. "How did you come to be in Salzburg, if I may ask?"

"I came here for love. Unfortunately, it didn't end as a children's tale."

"Oh, I wouldn't say I came here for love, exactly." The duchess gives Josef a look that is lost on him.

Anna considers what kind of woman marries without love.

The duchess carries on. "I couldn't help notice you've been without a cane of late. You've recovered from your accident, then?”

“Yes, madam. I am on the mend.”

“That’s lovely to hear. You took a trip recently, didn’t you? Home to see your family?”

“I did.”

“You miss them.”

“At times.”

“But you won’t be leaving Salzburg.”

“Not likely.”

“I can’t help but wonder what it is that keeps you here. If you came for a love now lost, why do you stay?”

Anna gives Josef a look. “This is my home now.”

The clockmaker continues to eat, oblivious to the scrutiny from the two women, who then look at each other and laugh. It is their mutual giggling that finally draws him from his meal.

“A joke?” he asks.

“No, my darling,” Klara tells him. “It’s nothing.”

Anna raises an eyebrow at the endearment.

Josef turns to her. “I must say, this beef is sublime.”

“Thank you,” she replies.

The three continue their dining in silence.

While Klara finds Josef's distracted manner charming, Anna is concerned. She knows all-too-well that his absent-minded tendencies indicate he is having difficulty with a project. Once the duchess has left for the day, Anna enters Josef's study, where he hunkers over his worktable, head in one hand, fraying quill pen in the other. She refreshes the current candles and lights more. She brings him the ubiquitous cup of chocolate, then stands near and watches.

Where she ached to take someone—anyone—to bed with her, she longs at this moment for it to be Josef. She believes he alone would accept her as she is. Doesn't he need a respite from the weight his work that keeps him occupied night after lonely night? No matter what he may think Klara can give him, Anna feels she herself is the one to rescue him. Just as he rescued her. She reaches out to touch his shoulder.

"Yes?" he finally says.

Before the warmth of her palm makes contact, she looks upon the drawings on the table. She's seen those lines before; the images and dimensions are familiar. She pulls her hand back.

"You're working on another heart?"

"Yes. This one has been commissioned by the duke," Josef says. "It seems Leopold Brunner and I share more than I'd care to admit. A general dislike of people, bad hearts—"

"The duchess."

Josef's glare sends a chill down Anna's back.

She shakes her head. "I'm sorry—I—I didn't mean…"

"Was there something you needed?"

"I was wondering what I could do to you—I mean, what I could do to *assist* you. How can I help?"

Josef shakes his head before resting it back on his hand. He scratches down a note, squeezing illegible phrases between smudged calculations.

"You're in need of a new pen," she tells him. "I'll pick one up for you in the morning. I'll acquire some new notebooks as well."

He nods without a word.

"Josef?"

"Yes?"

"What can I do?"

The clockmaker stops and looks up. In a tone so heavy she almost doesn't hear him, he tells her, "You can leave me to my work, Anna."

Though disheartened, his response gives Anna an idea. The next day, she does something she thought she would never do and asks the duchess for help. Before Josef can realize she's arrived, Anna stops Klara at the front of the shop.

"Yes, he does seem particularly discouraged about his work," Klara says in response to Anna's elucidation of Josef's despondency. "I took it to be a normal condition of his process."

"It is not normal to this extent," explains Anna. "There's a greater responsibility this time—the urgency of saving your husband's life."

Klara nods.

"The husband you don't love."

The duchess pulls back. "That seems irrelevant."

Anna bows. "Yes, it is. I apologize, madam. I meant no disrespect or criticism."

"Yes, Josef and I are fond of each other, but we're not ghouls plotting the duke's death. The very fact that he's dedicating so much of himself to save my husband's life is merely one more thing that endears Josef to me. You know as well as I do what a unique man he is."

"Again, madam, I apologize." Anna bows again. "What I'm trying so poorly to say is that Herr Kronecker functions better without distractions."

"You think I should leave him alone, so he can work."

"Yes."

The duchess turns the idea over in her head, her eyes on the closed door of the clockmaker's study. "You may be right. I've been selfish."

"It's not that."

"That's what I've been, isn't it?" Klara frowns. "A selfish distraction."

"The finest distraction, madam."

Klara smiles sadly. "Every man needs a woman in his life. It seems Herr Kronecker is fortunate enough to have two." She reaches out to take Anna's right hand, but Anna tactfully turns to offer her left. The duchess leaves before Josef can see she's there and does not come back the next day.

Someone else, however, does. Elias Dorn. His return clouds the shop more than the overcast afternoon.

"What could you possibly have left to say to me?"

Anna offers him nothing else in the form of a greeting, but instead waits, void of emotion as he squirms to compose himself.

"I've slept little since…"

Her lips curl at his weary pause. "Perhaps you should try some laudanum."

As she turns away, Elias finds his voice. "I've prayed for you—for what happened to you and for the wisdom of what I must do."

"There's nothing you must do," Anna tells him. "Except go away and stay away."

"I can't."

Annoyed yet curious, Anna moves toward him. One step, then two steps. "Why?"

Elias finally notices. "Your legs. What happened? You're—walking. Where's your cane?"

Anna cannot contain her delight at Elias's pained confusion. She grins with teasing vindication. "It's a miracle. I'm cured."

The priest cowers at her laugh. "Show me your legs. Somewhere private, if you like."

"No," Josef tells him as he emerges from his study. "She will not indulge your perverse impropriety."

"The perversity is here, Herr Kronecker." Elias gestures around the shop. Then, to Anna, "I insist."

Josef glares. "I insist you leave."

"I'll consent," Anna says. "There will be no need for a private room. The light in here is best."

Josef gives in with a resigned sigh.

Once she's sure Elias is looking down at her legs, Anna lifts up her dress, just to her knees. She didn't agree to expose her legs where she stands because of the *abundance* of light, but because, as she said, the light in here is *best*. Best for her purpose, that is. With just the right illumination the leggings of wool, gold, and silver that cover her clockwork appendages possess a very human appearance—one similar in tone and texture to her own skin—as long as she isn't examined too closely. After a moment, she lets the hem of her dress fall back to her feet.

"Satisfied?" says Josef, doing all he can to contain his spiteful elation. "You've gone astray, Father. You need to find your way back to the flock. Heed what Bishop von Bohn has to teach you."

Elias attempts to straighten his defeated posture but fails. "Perhaps I should find my way to the *arch*bishop, instead."

"As you like. You can begin by leaving my shop."

Elias departs. Anna watches with relief, while Josef does so with great scrutiny.

"He's become a thorn in an unreachable place," the clockmaker says.

"I'm sorry, Josef. For all this."

"A trifle, really." He turns with a shrug, then back. "Has there been any word from Duchess Brunner?"

Anna shakes her head. He turns once more and starts for his study. She watches him drag behind him the gravity of the duke's health, the absence of Klara, and now the judgement of an obtuse priest. "The forger promised parts later today," she manages to say with a hint of optimism.

"No later than yesterday would've been preferred."

They have dinner in silence. The ticking clocks measure the tension rather than soothe it. That evening, she decides to give Josef the gift she's been putting off. From her room, she retrieves a small painted box and takes it tentatively to his study. The clockmaker spins at the creak of the floor beneath her step. The sight of Anna deflates his obvious hope, and his expression settles back into a scowl.

"No," she tells him. "I am not the duchess."

"Of course." Josef sighs, his gaze lost. "I just thought…"

Unable to endure the sight of him hunched over his table any longer, Anna takes his arm with her left hand, while her right clasps the gift behind her back. She leads him to the sofa. Josef's energies are so spent that he allows himself to be coaxed across the room. He collapses on the upholstered cushion. With graceful ease, Anna sits next to him. She does not feel it, but as her knee presses against his, he rests his hand upon it.

"There is something wrong in the forging of the parts," Josef confesses with weary eyes. "Either that or my calculations are amiss. If I have not made the correct estimations regarding the duke's weight and stature—"

"Then the mechanized pump would be no more effective than his current heart. The duke's life expectancy would be no better. Possibly even less."

"Yes."

Anna's hand moves up his arm to his shoulder. "You need to move forward by starting over. If you question your calculations or the forger's work or anything at all, you need to scrap it and begin anew. You know that. You would have wasted far less time if you'd done it days ago."

Josef straightens. His fleeting respite gives way to renewed agitation. He rubs his eyes. "I can't." His stare penetrates the walls as he searches around the room. "What has happened to Klara?"

Anna's hand drops to her side. "The duchess and I—we thought it best if you were left to your work, without the hindrance of another's company."

"We?"

"Well…yes."

"Why would you think that is your decision to make?"

His tone stops her, but only a moment. "As your assistant, I think it is my place to make sure you keep working. Without—"

"You don't think starting over would be a hinderance? And what is this?" Josef stands, gesturing to Anna's presence on the couch and the box behind her back. "What do you have there? What else are you keeping from me?"

She gives a hopeless groan and hands him the gift.

He opens it. "What are these?"

Mustering the cheeriest tone she can, Anna says, "Eyes. For Joop."

"They're rocks."

"They're crystals. Rainbow Moonstones. See how they reflect the light?"

Each stone has been cut and set within a sphere of fine, white marble, and a piece of polished onyx has been set within each stone. Josef takes one of the perfectly smooth, brilliant balls in his fingers as though he were touching feces. Anna's stomach tightens.

"I—wanted—crystal," the clockmaker says, his voice low.

"I think they are quite beautiful. The colors are remarkable."

"*Crystal!*" Josef shouts at Anna. "As in *glass*. Not stones!"

Anna flinches. "I'm—"

"Since when can you not follow the simplest request?"

"—sorry."

"You claim to be my assistant? Then *assist* me! I

need help, not empty-headed carelessness."

Anna stands and drops the box with the remaining stone at his feet. "Go to hell."

With a swiftness that startles Josef, Anna leaves the study and hurries from the shop just as Christoph is entering. The momentum of her powerful legs pushes her past him with ease.

"Anna," the doctor calls after her, "you've forgotten your coat!"

ELEVEN

...AND ANOTHER FATEFUL MEETING

Anna finds herself wandering narrow alleys as foreboding as the arriving winter; with every snow-crunching step she takes, the city grows colder and darker. If she had been of rational mind when she left Kronecker's, she might have reconsidered her decision and found a warm place indoors in which to collect herself, but all she knew was she had to get away.

Josef's outrage plays over in her head and pounds in her temples, its intensity undiminished by the distance she puts between herself and the shop, thumping ever greater the farther she gets or the faster she walks. Her breath burns the night air. The fog of each exhalation wraps itself around her face and shoulders. She becomes disorientated, and it's not long before she is lost.

"Damn it to hell."

Anna is as guilty as anyone to fall under love's foolish spell. It brought her to Salzburg, and it's the very reason she's lost now. None the wiser. Only colder.

She looks for places she's visited before: the gem-cutter, the purveyor of fine timepieces, the chocolatier, anything to help her orientate herself. But one lane of businesses after another looks the same and unfamiliar.

Until she comes upon a home that strikes her as familiar. It's something about the pair of lions sitting nobly and statuesque on either side of the grand, glass doors. Something in the light from inside that casts shadows of people sharing an evening of gaiety. She wanders along a cobblestone lane beside the home. Broken pieces of her memory tease her, distract her from the cold. Then she finds herself looking down a rocky ravine.

Damn it to hell.

She really shouldn't recognize it, considering the near-dead, incoherent state she was in the first time. Yet, there it is. Her once final resting place. The grave of stones from which she was resurrected.

Anna turns and walks back up the lane. She knows whose house it is now.

"We should look for her," Christoph tells Josef almost a half an hour after Anna ran off.

"Of course we should." Josef dons a coat. "Leave the door unlatched in case she returns."

"*When* she returns. One way or another, she'll be safe in her bed come morning."

"I'm such a fool," Josef mutters.

"Yes. And an ass."

Anna has no idea how long she's been outside the house with the lion statues. She doesn't watch so much as listen. She wants to hear that laugh. It's the only way she'll truly be sure. Just the memory of it curdles her blood. To hear it again would bring it to boil.

The occasional passerby peers at her, unsure what to think of what their eyes behold—a woman underdressed for the cold, steam rising from her heated body, her misty breath thrusting from her mouth like fire from a dragon. No one dares pass too near the burning woman. However, a servant who'd been watching her through the glass doors warily steps outside. Through the briefly opened door, Anna hears it—the cursed laugh of the demon.

The look on Anna's face stops the servant faster than the air's chill. "Can I assist you somehow, Fräulein?" he asks.

Without hesitation, she answers, "The count is expecting me. A private invitation."

The young servant gives her a look that says, *Of course, that explains everything.* He motions for Anna to follow him inside.

Her nose wrinkles at the air heavy with rum, wine, and body odor. It's apparent the throng of guests has been at it for some time, sealed from the winter night, lost in their own frivolous, drunken merriment. None of them pays Anna any mind as she is led up a flight of stairs and down a long hall to a door painted gold and white. Anna gives not a moment of reflection to the fact that she ascended the stairs with grace and ease. Inside the darkened room, the servant begins to light candles.

"Not too many," Anna tells him.

The servant nods, thinking he wouldn't want to look upon the count too much or too closely, either— intimately or otherwise.

"Shall I start a fire?" he asks her.

"No. I shouldn't be long."

The servant gives a knowing chuckle before exiting. Anna shudders at what it is the young man thinks he knows. Alone, she looks about the room. Nothing is familiar. It is not the room where she was beaten and raped. *Murdered and defiled.* That happened downstairs, shortly after beginning her servitude to the count. The beast had wasted no time in forcing himself upon her. Her previous masters had at least allowed her to be of some use cleaning or cooking first. But not this count. He had taken her in specifically for his carnal needs.

The sound of something against the door startles her. Or rather, awakens her. *What the hell am I doing here?*

The door opens, and the Count enters with stumbling steps. Even without knowing what she does about the man, she couldn't see him as anything but vile. His mere presence reeks of unpleasantness. Although Anna stands before him like a gift-wrapped offering, the count makes no attempt to straighten his frayed wig, smooth his disheveled silk banyan, or use it to cover the stains spotting his ruffled shirt underneath. Anna cringes to imagine what those stains are.

"Fräulein." The count voice is thick and slurred

with alcohol. "For what do I owe this pleasure?" He takes an unbalanced step forward, just enough to lean against a pedestal, on which rests a bust of some dead philosopher—not unlike the one he used to break her legs. He releases a belching hiccup. "Or is it you who owes me the pleasure?"

Anna moves closer to the light of a candle. "You don't remember me?"

His brows raise at the sight of her crooked features, but a lecherous grin curls his crusted lips upon seeing her heated complexion. Still, his face twists with incomprehension.

"Have you left so many women for dead that you couldn't possibly recall one from another?"

"So it's riddles you've come to play?"

"No, my lord, I've not come with humor."

"I've had enough of games this evening. Unless you've come here to be wheelbarrowed, you may leave." He shoos her as if she were nothing more than an insect and turns to leave.

Anna pounces. The powerful springs of her legs send her across the room and onto the count's back. Even in his drunken state, she is unable to take his girth to the floor. He spins, and she slips from him and against the door with a thud. As she falls, she is able to dig the nails of her left fingers deep into his fleshy cheek.

The count lets out a yelp like a spanked child. He touches a hand to his face, and warm fluid coats his palm. In the dim light, his own blood shimmers on his fingers. His arrogance melts to confusion—and then fear. He finally *sees* Anna as she stands with a fierce, animalistic look of survival on her face. He remembers. Before he can scream for help, Anna puts her right hand at his throat. She presses her weight into him, backing him against a teetering side table. His attempted shout comes out as a muffled squeak. "You? But... I..."

"Thought I was dead?" Anna finishes his thought in a fiery whisper. "I'm so glad you haven't broken so many legs that you would forget mine. I'm flattered."

"How—"

"Did I find you?"

The count shakes his head and looks down to the lower half of her body.

"How am I standing here when I should be without legs?"

He nods.

"*I have no legs*, thanks to you. I am a legless miracle of science. A divine creation of man. Some men giveth what other men taketh away." She leans farther into the count to punctuate her words.

As his feet slip, the count grabs her hand pressed against his throat. His eyes open wider when he feels its steel hardness. He shudders. The distinct odor of urine wafts upward.

Anna glances down to see the wet stain pooling in his breeches, and she can't help but laugh. "Do you think I've come here to kill you?"

The count doesn't move. The terror in his eyes is Anna's satisfying answer.

"I'm not sure why I've come here tonight. It certainly wasn't my intention. Just fate, really. Delicious, malevolent fate having a little fun with the two of us."

The count swallows and tries to speak, yet nothing comes out.

"I'm not here to kill you. I'd much rather let you live with the memory of this moment. I'll leave you with the knowledge that I am out there, somewhere, able to return at any time. You'll never, ever forget me again.

Maybe I'll return." She lets out a beastly little laugh of her own. "Or maybe I won't." Then she shrugs.

It is here that fate steps in with a bit more fun, for Anna is wound so tightly with rage and vindication that her shrug comes off more like a—twitch—and her hand snaps shut around the count's throat.

Her eyes open wide. The count gurgles and struggles for air. She yanks her arm back in surprise, but her hand is still closed and tears flesh from the count as it comes away. He collapses, clutching at his opened throat. His eyes swell with each desperate attempt to breathe. Anna can see in the candlelight his pale-white complexion turning a dark blue. His body convulses in its fight for oxygen. As blood trickles from his mouth, so does life leave his body.

Anna looks down at the count, as still and silent as the fallen snow outside. She wants to scream, to laugh, to cry, to cheer. She stands over him in triumph yet shakes with fear at what she's done. The realization of her predicament hits her. The count's body blocks the only way out. She shouldn't leave the way she came anyway, past the watchful eyes of the servants. Taking deep, rhythmic breaths to quell her panic, Anna devises a simple plan: the balcony.

Her burning vehemence is smacked hard by the night air as she opens the French doors. Severe shivering engulfs her body. She composes herself enough to step out onto the narrow balcony and close the doors behind her. She looks over the iron railing. Two stories down and snow to land on. Before the shivering shakes can take over again, Anna clumsily lifts herself over the railing, then she drops to the ground below.

Her legs easily absorb the weight of the landing. However, her body, within its hard, glass cradle, suffers the blow of gravity. The air is knocked out of her. She cringes in winded agony. She might have blacked out, had it not been for her chattering jaw stimulating her consciousness. The pain subsides. Her thoughts clear as she resumes breathing and she looks around to see if anyone witnessed her plummet. Seeing the lane is empty, Anna hurries in a direction she hopes will lead her home.

Against Josef's preference, Christoph hails a carriage to aid in their search.

"We'll be able to cover more ground this way," the doctor says, "and avoid freezing to death in the process."

Josef's preoccupation with the search hinders a response. He doesn't expect to see Anna so much as spot a clue as to where she might have gone.

"Besides," Christoph continues, "when we find her, there's a chance she'll be in need of medical attention. I don't imagine either one of us could carry her very far for very long."

"That's assuming she's even outside," Josef finally replies. "Who's to say she hasn't taken refuge beside a fire with a stein of warm mead, contentedly cursing me."

Christoph laughs. "It would be like her to do that, wouldn't it? I'll tell the driver to stop at all the taverns he knows of."

※   ※

When Anna finally finds her way back to Kronecker's she is shaking so uncontrollably that she must strain to move her legs. The hot fire of her vengeance does little to heat her cold skin. Her foot catches on a cobblestone as she nears the door, and she falls.

Of Gilded Flesh / 230

But someone is there to catch her. His lean arms pull her into an embrace that is both compassionate and unyielding. He eases her shaking body to the floor inside the shop with the gentlest of strength. She can't help but melt into him, her contours conforming to his.

"My God, Anna, you're freezing. What were you thinking?" he whispers, and his voice pierces her delirium.

"P-P-Pascal?" Anna manages. "W-What are y-you…"

"They sent word you had gone missing." He rubs his hand over her bare arm. "I searched for you, then came here in hopes you had returned."

She looks up to see his dark hair cascading down along the sides of his deep-set eyes. Her gaze traces the lines of his Romanesque features. No longer is he the boy maestro. Still young, yes, but now a man. Anna wants to return his embrace—if she could just stop the infernal shivering.

Pascal loosens his arms around her. "Let me get you a blanket or a cloak."

"N-N-No! S-Stay!"

"You need to be wrapped up."

The heat of her crime ignites the need that's been smoldering within her. It rises to the surface and thaws her chill. "N-No. I so desperately need someone, Pascal. Will *you* be my cloak tonight?" Her previously icy lips, now hot as coals, meet his. He turns, moving to pick her up.

"Wait." She grabs his shoulder with her left hand. "You have to know something."

Anna doesn't feel the weight of his hand on her steel knee or his caress upon her thigh through her silken dress. But she does see the truth in his eyes. Through her own tearing, blurred sight, she sees the understanding on his face.

"I know your secret, Anna. I figured it out." He presses his palm to her bodice, feeling the hard, porcelain surface underneath. Then, in a seamless, singular motion, he lifts her from the floor and tells her, "It doesn't matter."

With Anna in his arms, Pascal negotiates the maze of shadowed displays. They enter her room. She reaches out, closes the door, and locks it. Flames are already crackling in the fireplace.

"You've been waiting for me?" she asks.

"Of course." He puts her feet onto the floor. "Josef and Christoph went out to look for you. Now I have you to myself."

He raises her right arm and removes the fleshy glove from her hand. Then he removes her hand and does the same with his left. He tugs at her bodice string, but its slack resistance keeps it from untying.

Anna giggles. She takes the other end in her fingers. "Allow me to assist."

Together, with their opposite, single hands, they work to loosen her clothing until it falls into a crumpled pile at her feet.

At the sight of her, Pascal's mouth falls open. "Amazing."

She looks down at her legs. "Yes. Herr Kronecker surpassed himself with these."

"I'm not talking about those."

Anna looks back up to see that Pascal is looking at *her*—her body, her face—taking her all in. She puts her hand over her left eye and an arm across her chest at the sudden realization that she is naked and exposed before him.

"I don't know what I was thinking," she says.

"How can you bear to…" She looks away, now unable to meet his tender gaze.

Pascal takes her hand and moves it from her face, then turns to the fire. "That hearth," he whispers. "I don't see it as cracked, cold stone. There is beauty in its texture, and even more in the glow and warmth that emanates from it. The light it gives. How easy it is to get lost in those flames." He looks, again, to her. "You are like firelight, Anna. I'm drawn to your glow. Your warmth gives me peace. I lose myself in you when you're near." He puts his palm against her thin, muscular stomach. She catches her breath. Surrendering to his touch, she finally brings her eyes to his and finds solace there. Pascal pulls back with a quizzical frown at the glass urn Anna's torso rests within.

"What is it?" she asks.

"How do you…? Do you hop out of there…or…?"

She laughs, and so does he. "We have to loosen these…" She indicates a set of straps on either side of her waist and works to slacken their attachment to her. Pascal helps as best he can. Once the straps fall away, Anna raises her arms for him to lift her from her porcelain cradle.

He moves in as close as he can, slipping his right hand under her left arm and the end of his left under her right. He raises her up and helps her onto the bed. Anna props herself on her elbows as she watches him undress, admiring his taut physique—the body of a fencer, not a pianist. He strips down without taking his eyes from her. His longing for her is so genuine that she finds herself looking shyly away again. Then she laughs, which prompts Pascal to look at what has her attention. It's the clockwork legs with their glass bowl atop. He sees the humor in the eccentric image as well, the misaligned art of a steel sculpture standing comically near a man and a woman about to make love.

They turn back to one another. Completely unclothed now, Pascal lays himself over her. They kiss. Anna runs her hand over him. Everything about him is firm with youth—his arms, his shoulders, his back, his hips. Everything, she muses with a giggle, is like the hardened steel of Marquis de Castile's phallus.

Pascal leans away to look down at her. "What is funny?"

"Nothing," she tells him, moving her hand to his

face. "Please, don't stop."

He sighs. "I feel I must or I will be done too soon."

"Then slow down, but don't stop."

For minutes that seem like hours, they consume each other, finding that lover's rhythm, that passionate harmony, until finally clasping each other in a mutual wave of bliss.

They hold each other, their collective breath the only sound in the quiet firelight.

TWELVE

Of

MISGUIDED POETS

Anna doesn't sleep. With Pascal warm beside her under the covers, she watches the fire, which has burned down to glowing embers. They made love twice more before he drifted off.

She heard Josef and Christoph return to the shop at one point in the night. They tried her door. Finding it locked, the two made the conclusion that she had come back and secluded herself there for privacy.

"For the best," she heard Christoph say.

"For the time being," was Josef's response.

Now, as the light of morning creeps through her window, Anna listens for other voices—those of the authorities come to take her away for murder or simply the voice of Josef, at the door, offering apologies. Yet only the silence of dawn touches her senses.

Knowing she won't be falling back to sleep, Anna

decides to ready herself for the day. Or she would if she could get to her damn legs. She is not typically lifted from her porcelain cradle and carried to bed. The legs would normally stand directly at her bedside and she'd climb in and out of them with relative ease. Now, they are just out of reach. She stretches as far as she can without tumbling from the bed. Then she feels hands upon her, and arms wrapping around her, lifting her from the soft linens.

"Allow me," Pascal tells her, his breath upon her neck, his bare flesh against hers.

She stops him. "I need to relieve myself."

"Of course." He carries her to a far corner of the room, where a chamber pot rests next to a basin of water on the floor. A sturdy wooden frame wraps around the pot, allowing Anna to support herself.

"I'll take it from here," she says.

"Of course."

When she's done, Pascal takes her in his arms again. "Shall I bathe you?"

She laughs. "If you must."

He gently sets her in a basin. Sponge in hand, he kisses her. The heat of his mouth offsets the cold of the water trickling down her shoulders, back, and breasts. He touches the wet sponge to her goosebumps.

With a curious smile, she asks, "When did you freshen the water?"

"Last night. I anticipated you might need cleansing when you returned. And a warm fire."

"You think of everything, apparently."

"When it comes to you, yes."

"I fear you think of me too much."

He sets the sponge aside and finds a towel. He wraps it around Anna as he lifts her once more. Once she's dry, he places her into the urn upon her legs.

"You should lie back down," she tells him.

With an impish smirk, he leaps onto the mattress and covers his lower body with blankets. The youthful, supple lines of his chest and arms tease her to rejoin him under the covers.

She smiles. "You should sleep."

"I'd rather watch you dress."

Anna avoids his gaze while she ties herself into her garments. Whether his feelings for her are genuine and hers for him are not, or her feelings for him *are* sincere and she fears to accept them, Anna can't say.

She's not yet ready to address either possibility. Once she's dressed, she tells him again, "You should sleep," then leaves the room.

The clinking of tools and the orange light of candles trail from the workroom in the back of the shop. Anna enters the space through the open curtain. She knows full well it is Josef working within. Expecting to see him hovering over Duke Brunner's heart, she's surprised to find the clockmaker tinkering with Joop instead. He's inserting the Rainbow Moonstone-and-marble balls into the vacant eye sockets. Anna's own eyes tighten to squeeze back tears. *The dear, insufferable man.* Having come to know him so well, she knows that, in Josef Kronecker's unique way, he is apologizing.

The clockmaker leans back and moves a burning candle from one side of Joop's head to the other. He steps back. "Come see," he says.

Anna moves to Josef's side—close to him, but not too close.

"They catch the light with such brilliance," he says. "So much more lifelike than what I first imagined." He returns the candle to its place on a shelf. "Thank you, Anna."

She gives him a smile.

"You were right about something else, too," he says.

"What's that?"

"I do need to start over. The duke's heart is a mess."

"That is no doing of yours. The one you're making for him will be a vast improvement."

Josef laughs. He reaches for her hand, yet she finds herself pulling away. Piano music comes from the other side of the shop and hovers between the two of them. Josef gives a curious look.

"Pascal is here already?"

"Actually," Anna says, "he came by last night...and never left."

Josef turns to her, taking in the warmth she emits like a gently burning hearth. "I see." He turns away.

"I'll bring you a cup momentarily."

He nods then disappears into the darkness of the shop.

Anna moves closer to Joop and rests her left hand beside him. To get a better look into his newly acquired eyes, she lowers herself to a stool, which creaks under her weight.

"Oh, Joop. What have I done?"

The boy stares vacantly back as a tear rolls down her cheek.

"I killed a man. He was so very horrible—a demon—but who am I to pass judgement and execution? My vengeance has made me no better."

Another tear falls.

"I'm worse, even. For I've gone and lain myself with a man I do not love."

One of Joop's hands slips from his lap and rests upon hers. The comforting, humanlike gesture from the unhuman boy sparks a faint grin on her lips and then a flood of tears.

"And worse still…I want to again."

⊕ ❧ ⊕ ❧ ⊕

One thought above all others shadows Anna's morning. It is not Pascal's touch upon her or her conflicted emotions. It is the death of the count—her *murder* of the count. She argues with herself that was an accident and comes to realize that it is not remorse that eats at her, but the consequences.

Not for herself.

But for Josef and Christoph.

If she were caught and tried, and the nature of her mechanized physicality came to light, would the clockmaker and the doctor be considered accomplices in her heinous crime? Anna would most likely be hanged, and the careers and lives of those dear men could be ruined. *A fate worse than death,* she believes. Anna's fear is such that she finds herself trembling when Dr. Baeder arrives later in the day. She eavesdrops on their conversation in the study.

"…the strangest of occurrences. I must tell you about it," Christoph says.

"Yes? What is it?" Josef asks.

"I was asked earlier today to examine the body of one Count Adolf Hirsch."

Hirsch. Anna's heart races at hearing his name.

"Having only met him once, I found him a most loathsome man. Now he is dead, and just as loathsome."

"What is so strange about that?"

"His throat was ripped from him." Anna does not see, but the doctor illustrates with his right hand to his own throat, showing Josef how that might have appeared. "He drowned in his own blood."

"That is strange," Josef agrees.

"It becomes stranger. One of his servants…"

Anna holds her breath.

"…he claims to have seen an apparition enter the room with the Count."

"A ghost?"

"He swears upon it, because he never saw this so-called phantom leave the room. With no other way out, he claims the murderous specter vanished into the night."

"A window, perhaps?"

"An upper story. Much too great a drop."

The two sigh, then chuckle in dismay at the very peculiar account of Count Hirsch's demise. What Anna doesn't hear in the lull of conversation is Josef's consideration of the unnatural strength it must take to tear a man's throat out, and where this train of thought is leading him before being interrupted by Christoph.

"How progresses your work here?" the doctor asks.

"Not as well as I'd like."

"It's never as well as you'd like."

"True." Josef concedes. "What of the duke's condition?"

"Not as well as *I'd* like. He took a bad turn this morning."

Anna does not linger to hear the rest. She forces herself from the vicinity of Josef's study within a twisted eddy of guilt, elation, disgust, and unsettling gratification.

❦   ❦   ❦

Klara Brunner watches her husband drift into deep, recuperative slumber. She sits upon an armless side chair, its back and legs made of gilded walnut. Not exactly a seat meant for comfort, but then the duchess is not there to be comfortable. She watches and waits in the hope that each snorting inhalation will be the duke's last. With every breath he takes, however, her anticipation becomes disappointment. So fixated is she on her growing discontentment that she doesn't notice Herr Weisman's entrance. She turns with a start when he speaks.

"The way he hangs on, it's almost as though he has something to live for. But whatever could that be?"

Klara glares at the little man with the greatest of annoyance.

"There is great power in hope, isn't there?" Weisman continues. "Hope of what may lie ahead. There's an inexplicable magic, wouldn't you say, in how one can keep going despite the odds. It's inspiring. Infectious. I can't help but admire his tenacity."

"Sometimes I wonder whose side you're on."

"I am on the side of whomever I serve."

The duchess sighs and shakes her head. "How opportunistic of you."

"For you, ma'am, I am like anyone else who becomes entrapped by your secret: at your mercy."

Ignoring his insolence, Klara stands with renewed conviction. "I think it is time I returned to the clockmaker's side."

● ❧ ● ❧ ●

In the days to follow, Anna's agitated state supersedes all else. Even the resumed presence of Duchess Brunner—the women's brief alliance apparently forgotten—has little effect on her. Klara spends more time than ever with Josef.

Of Gilded Flesh / 246

Pascal's presence increases as well. Besides filling the shop with music, he finds he has a knack for tinkering with clocks and helps with simple repairs. He also "tinkers" with Anna every chance he gets, and she welcomes the distraction.

If the two of them could spy into the clockmaker's studio, they would probably find Josef and Klara's company together clumsy, if not sadly humorous—Josef working diligently at his desk, Klara sitting across the room with a book or a copy of the Viennese newspaper *Wiener Zeitung* in hand, eyeing him for any opportune moment to interrupt his work.

Looking about the room one day, Klara says, "This space needs something to make it less…stuffy. A painting, perhaps. Or a portrait of me. I have plenty." She gives a wry grin.

Josef glances about. "There'd be no place to hang it. You'd end up here behind my table with the others." He gestures to dusty artwork leaning against the wall.

Another time, she inquires, "How did you come to make mechanical body parts?"

"I attended medical university for a time," Josef explains without looking at her. "That's how I met

Christoph. But while I've always been fascinated by the science of the human body, I found the inner workings of clocks much more to my liking—as well as their company. I much prefer the ticking of a clock over the chattering of humans any day."

"I've never understood misanthropes. I mean, humans aren't all bad. We all like *someone*. You like Christoph, Herr Künzi, and Annamarie. You like me, don't you?"

"Perhaps it is a matter of numbers. I tolerate individuals. It's *people* I find torturous."

"Oh, so you find me tolerable."

"Only just," Josef says with a sideways glance and grin.

On another day, Klara asks, "How did you come to have a woman as an assistant? It seems a unique arrangement."

"Anna is a unique woman."

"I've gathered that."

"She needed work, and I needed an assistant. Our arrangement is symbiotic."

Klara sighs. "Do you love her?"

"I suppose, in a sense. We've shared an eventful

couple of years. We've relied on each other."

Klara's exasperation finally gets the best of her. "Are you *in love* with her, Josef?"

"I wouldn't—"

"She's in love with you. Are you aware?"

Josef faces the duchess. Then he looks to the wall his study shares with Anna's bedroom. A trace of melancholy colors his voice. "She has an interesting way of showing it."

"You mean Pascal? He's merely a frolic. Sometimes, a woman just needs a man's attention."

"We're still talking about Anna, aren't we?"

Klara scowls. "You can be such an ass."

It's a couple of days before the duchess returns to the shop. When she does, she sits on the sofa, nearer to Josef than usual.

"Have you ever been married?" she asks.

Josef's silence makes Klara wonder if he heard her. Just when she's about to ask again, he replies, "Once. Years ago."

"Children?"

"A son." Before she can follow with the next, obvious question, Josef stops working and tells her,

"They died in a carriage accident. He was five. A day doesn't go by that I don't think about them. Was there anything else? I need to get back to my work." He turns his attention back to his drawings.

Klara nods. "That explains the mechanical boy."

"It explains nothing."

"You had five years with him. That's more than many can say." She leans in. "I will never know that feeling, Josef. I can never have children."

Josef doesn't look at her. "Perhaps with your next husband."

"No. The fault is mine, not Leopold's. I am infertile. I…I've gone to great lengths to keep it from him. At first, to save his pride. Now, as the lie has gone on so long, to keep my life. He would surely behead me if he were to ever learn the truth."

He looks at her now with a question in his eyes: *why are you telling me this?*

She reaches a hand to his arm. "I wanted you to know. I trust you."

Josef smiles curiously, sadly, before turning back to his desk.

Klara allows him to work for a time before she

asks, "How does your heart know when to increase or slow its rate in response to physical activity?"

"That's a good question." Josef indicates his drawings to illustrate. "The answer is in the question. There's a kind of pendulum…here"—he points—"a balance that moves in response to movement of the body. That balance regulates the pace at which the mechanism pumps blood through the body. It's a similar principle that allows the heart to wind itself. To a certain degree, that is."

Klara stands and moves closer to Josef.

He continues, "The challenge I'm having with your husba—with Duke Brunner—is his size. Or rather, his thickness. I fear the mechanism will have difficulty sensing his movement in the appropriate manner. I would hate to give him a new heart that works just enough to keep him alive. I don't want to condemn him to a life of only sitting or lying still."

"It would not be much different, I'm afraid." Klara leans over the table, her shoulder against Josef's. "What about an increased heart rate from an emotional influence?"

"Like anger or fear?"

"For example."

"One's increased respiration," Josef says, catching the movement of Klara's chest as she breaths. "The lungs being so near the heart creates a similar effect."

"What about love? How does a heart of steel feel love?"

"That is a misguided vision of poets." Josef looks to Klara and shakes his head. "Love does not come from a bodily organ."

"From where, then, does it come?"

"I don't know. I just know one has nothing to do with the other."

"It sounds as though you are speaking from experience."

"I am."

"Josef?"

"Yes?"

"Why haven't you tried to lie with me?"

"You are married, Duchess."

Klara ignores the formal address. In a way, it entices her. She places a hand upon his arm. "We've been intimate with our eyes. With our words. We've shared our secrets. It only seems inevitable that we…"

Josef's response to her touch is tense and reticent.

"When was the last time you made love to a woman?"

He takes her hand from his arm but continues to hold it. "More years than I can remember."

She kisses his hand. "Perhaps I can refresh your memory."

Never has the calculating, centered clockmaker found his thoughts and desires in greater turmoil. He would rather it was Anna before him—he knows that— but Klara is so…

"You can try," is all he manages to say.

"Have you ever experienced fellatio?"

Josef's eyes widen as she kneels before him and loosens his breaches.

She snickers at his mute response. "I'll take that as a no."

The sensation of being taken by her is indescribable. He closes his eyes. He hears music. Klara then leads him to the sofa. Josef can tell she came prepared for this moment by the lack of layers beneath her dress. In particular, her pannier is missing, giving him ready access to her. But their lovemaking is fumbling and awkward. If Josef isn't haphazardly trying to maintain his balance upon Klara and the sofa, he's putting a hand in one place when she would rather have it in another. They seem unable to coordinate their mouths, missing each other's lips with graceless kisses. His irregular movement fails to match the steady motion of her hips.

Josef slides from atop Klara to sitting on the floor with an unfulfilled flop. Klara lies still, an arm dangling off the side of the sofa, equally unsatisfied. Their eyes look off to nothing, away from one another. The only sound is piano music from the other side of the wall.

In a voice as vacant as her gaze, Klara says, "I don't know that piece. It's quite nice."

"Yes," agrees Josef. "Quite."

※ ❧ ※ ❧ ※

On the other side of the wall, Anna lies in bed. Lingering intimacy warms her body as she watches Pascal at the piano. His one hand moves with such fluid agility that she swears he is playing with two. He's naked as he plays. She giggles at the sight of his sustained erection brushing against the base of the keyboard.

"Be careful you don't stain the finish."

Pascal looks down and laughs, yet continues to play.

"That's a beautiful piece," she tells him. "You've played that for me before, haven't you? I don't know its name."

"It is as yet unnamed," Pascal answers. "I wrote it for you a while ago."

"Just how long have you had feelings for me, anyway?"

"Thoughts of you have harbored within me since we first met."

"Harbored? More like festered, I'd say."

"More like nurtured, *I'd* say."

"I've made it no secret. I fear you think of me too much, Pascal. I wish I could tell you…" But Anna's doesn't know what she wishes she could tell him because she simply doesn't know what she feels anymore.

"Shhh, don't say anything. Just listen."

THIRTEEN

Of

BEASTLY SCHEMES

While Josef and Klara engage in their awkward interlude and Anna listens to her svelte, naked maestro play, the duke's health takes yet another turn for the worse. Fortunately, Dr. Baeder is there and performs emergency care as Herr Weisman scurries off for help— or rather, what *he* deems helpful. Some minutes later, he returns with Bishop von Bohn in tow. Leopold uses what little energy he has to wave his confidant from the room and declare, "I'm not dead yet, you imbecilic dolt."

"This agitation is exactly what you need to avoid," the bishop tells his brother.

"You'd be agitated, too, if you knew you were dying."

"Perhaps. But I am not dying, and neither are you."

The duke lays his head back in resignation. "You know damn well each breath I take could be my last." The silence from von Bohn and Dr. Baeder confirms the truth in what he says. "I can't wait any longer for the clockmaker. What is taking him so long?"

"He's ensuring your new heart is without imperfections," Christoph explains. "That takes time. He should be done soon."

"Soon is not soon enough." Brunner closes his eyes. His breathing settles to a restful cadence, and they suspect the duke is falling asleep. The bishop moves to show the doctor out, but Brunner opens his eyes. "I want you to transfer the clockmaker's heart into me."

"I'm sorry? What?"

"I want Josef Kronecker's heart. You can give him back his old one. It should keep him alive long enough for him to finish the one he's started for me, and then you can put that one into him."

"Absurd," the bishop sharply interjects.

"Is it?"

"You make it sound so simple," Christoph says. "There is nothing simple about this surgical procedure. It is extremely risky to have it done even once. You're suggesting Herr Kronecker go through it a third, even fourth time."

"But it will only be once for me."

Stunned, Christoph tells him, "I'll have no part of it."

The duke turns his head and sighs. "You're right, Doctor. I'm being selfish. I'm sorry." He closes his eyes. "I'm not being rational. Perhaps I just need to rest."

"Yes, perhaps."

"You may leave. I'm doing fine. Just tired."

Christoph bows. "Very well, then. I'll come back to check on you later." With a cautious nod to the bishop, he departs.

The duke's eyes open seconds later, alert and searching, only to be disappointed by the remaining presence of his brother.

"I am not surprised by your request," von Bohn tells him. "There are times that you are so much like—"

"Yes, yes," Leopold interrupts with an exasperated squirm. "I am cursed being our father's son, while you are blessed being our mother's."

"Curses and blessings have dictated our lives equally. The difference is a matter of how you choose to accept them—with grace or with contempt.”

“So now I am contemptible.”

“No, you are afraid.”

The duke responds with an impatient shake of his head.

“What is it that you want, brother, that you would risk another man’s life?” von Bohn asks.

“What every man wants, of course: to not die.”

“You will live. Just not in body. Immortality belongs to the soul.”

Nothing but brooding silence from Leopold.

“You’ve no reason to fear death.”

The duke brings his body upright as best he can. “I do not *fear* death. I’m just not ready for it. I’ve too much to do.” He falls back, his moment of strength already exhausted.

“What you need to do right now is rest.” The bishop moves to leave. Before closing the door behind him, he adds, “Please consider what I’ve said.”

“Yes. I will.”

Not a mere moment passes before Herr Weisman returns to the room.

“Matthew,” Leopold says, “summon Herr Zimic

here.”

“For what purpose would you need the likes of him?”

“That is not your concern. I simply need to speak with him.”

✦ ❧ ✦ ❧ ✦

Like the tangling, choking hold of lustrous devil’s ivy, a dichotomy of passion and trepidation infiltrates Kronecker’s. It grows and thickens in the dark. Anna finds herself dreading how much she longs for Pascal’s touch before days linger into night; while Josef cannot distract his own mind from Klara’s devilish allure.

Something is needed to lighten the shop’s sullen mood. A ball, perhaps. Costumes and dancing. Who better to put on such an event than the jovial Count Meusberger? It is the duchess who brings news of the dance to Josef.

“I don’t have time for such things,” he says. “I’m nearly done.”

“Yes, I know.” Klara puts a hand over his, stopping his work. “All the more reason you should take a moment for yourself. Enjoy an evening of frivolity.

Clear your mind before you finish. The duke is fine and resting. I assure you, he has many more days left."

Josef feigns a childish frown. "I loathe dancing."

"Why am I not surprised?" She gives him a kiss. "I should invite Anna and Pascal along, shouldn't I?"

⓪ ❧ ⓫ ❧ ⓯

"A ball?" Leopold Brunner reclines on his daybed.

Herr Weisman stands near. "Yes. Compliments of Count Meusberger."

The duke gives it the briefest consideration. "How convenient."

"My thoughts exactly. And we can thank your wife."

"Oh? How so?"

"It seems the duchess advised the Count in the matter."

"Really? What a dear. What would prompt her to do such a thing?"

"I've no idea. Does it matter?"

"I suppose not." The duke mulls this over. "We're sure Kronecker will be attending?"

"Yes."

"His assistant?"

"She is invited, as well."

"So no one will be in the shop?"

"That is my understanding."

After a little more consideration, the duke says, "Let Herr Zimic know, would you?"

"Of course." Herr Weisman bows before hurrying off.

Early in the evening before Meusberger's masquerade begins, Josef makes the last adjustments to Duke Brunner's heart. There is still a round of tests yet to be run, but he is confident enough in his work to say to himself, "It's done." And so, as he does at the completion of every project, the clockmaker steps to the couch, sits upon it with a kind of negotiated collapse and allows his body to meld into the cradling contours of the upholstery. He closes his eyes. Not to sleep, but to recollect the whole of the experience, like an epilogue to a lengthy tale.

He opens his eyes and looks about the room. Satisfied there are no lurking details waiting to vex him,

Josef empties his mind and listens. He takes in the soothing drone of the clocks—his livelihood, his life. He hears the murmur of voices. First Pascal's, then Anna's.

Anna.

He thinks not *What have I done?* for it is too late for that. *What now for us?* The clockmaker has never been one for regret; he acknowledges his mistakes—like taking an exceptional woman like Anna for granted—and then moves forward. The question now: Is there a way to move forward with her? Or is it too late?

His hand slips from his lap and falls upon a copy of *Wiener Zeitung* and news from Vienna. For something less emotionally taxing, he peruses the headlines and turns through pages, until he comes across an article on the strange, mysterious death of Count Adolf Hirsch here in Salzburg.

Again, he thinks of Anna.

🕐   🕐   🕐

Anna stands before a full-length giltwood mirror that is framed by a carving of coral honeysuckle in bloom. Pascal watches from an Italian chaise lounge. He wears nothing more than a bed shirt. Though he is not naked, he may as well be the way he sprawls and eyes Anna. She does her best to ignore him and gazes at the gown she wears. A dress of lavender and blue, its silhouette fits her form to perfection while exposing her shoulders and the elegance of her complexion.

"I don't believe I've ever seen anything lovelier," Pascal says.

Anna smiles. "The duchess gave me this. For tonight's dance."

"The Duchess Brunner?" he asks with suspicion.

"Yes. Why?"

"I never thought of the two of you as having a gift-giving kind of association."

Anna turns from one side to the other for a full view of the gown. She runs her left hand over the opposite sleeve made of sheer chiffon and lace. "I think she gave it to me as a kind of peace offering."

"A consolation prize? I thought that was me."

"Why do you say that?" Anna scowls. "You are no consolation."

"I'm not as naïve as you may think, Anna. Your feelings for Herr Kronecker have never been a secret."

"Then why would you take me as a lover?"

"Because my feelings for you are greater than either of yours for each other. I'm sure of it. I hope to convince you of that one day and change your mind." Pascal's bright tone drops just a little. "Unless, perhaps, I *am* naïve."

"You are not, my sweet," Anna says. "It is I who must convince myself. But, please, feel free to keep trying. You've been making some very strong arguments."

He laughs.

In an awkward attempt to change the subject, she asks, "Why aren't you getting dressed?"

"Wouldn't you rather stay? We'll have the entire shop to ourselves. Besides, I'm too tired to dance."

"Too tired to dance, but not too tired to strum me."

"How about we arrive later? I'm sure the affair will continue for some time."

Anna shakes her head. "You are incorrigible."

Pascal shrugs. He looks about the room and spies the fortepiano with a playful smirk. "Did you know there was time when Bach could not play his harpsichord?"

"No. Why was that?"

"It was Baroque."

Pascal laughs; Anna groans.

"A man walks into a tavern and orders an ale," he says. "To reach his money bag, the man must first remove a nine-inch-tall gentleman in fine clothing from his pocket. The bartender is amazed. The man explains, 'Yes. This little fellow is quite the musician. Plays a very small piano. He came into my possession when I once made a wish to a magical genie.' 'You wished for a nine-inch pianist?' the bartender asks. 'No, of course not.' the man says. 'The genie was hard of hearing.'"

Anna giggles—just a little. "Jokes? You're going to seduce me with jokes?"

"Is it working?"

She pauses. "Tell me another."

Pascal sits up. "A gentleman is about to make love to a countess when he looks with disappointment at the lack of hair between her legs. 'What is wrong?' she asks. He tells her, 'Grass does not grow on a well-trodden path.'"

This time, Anna truly laughs. "Are you sure she wasn't a *duchess?*"

Pascal jumps from the chaise and takes her in his

arms. "Now who's telling jokes?" Between kisses he tells her, "The last time I traveled to the East—I learned of a book—called the *Kamasutra*."

"You want to talk about books"—she pulls his shirt from him—"right now?"

"No—it is a book of"—he fumbles with the ties of her gown—"sensual love—and love-making."

"I see. And did you read it?"

"Cover to cover—and I have a very good memory."

There's a knock at the door. The lovers freeze.

"Anna?" comes Josef's voice. "May I come in?"

Pascal ducks behind the Coromandel screen as Anna answers, "Give me a moment." She tosses Pascal's shirt aside, unlocks the door, and allows Josef to enter.

The clockmaker looks upon his assistant as though seeing her for the very first time. He takes in the lavender lace of her dress, the porcelain splendor of her shoulders, the perfect imperfection of her face, and finds he can't remember what it was he wanted to speak to her about.

"Yes, Josef?"

"Is that what you'll be wearing this evening?"

She steps back, turning for him. "Yes. Do you like it?"

"I fear I would never get any work done if you were to wear that every day."

Anna blushes, averting her eyes. "This would be a rather silly thing to wear to clean clocks, wouldn't it?"

Josef gives a dry grin. "No, of course." He clears his throat. "I wonder if you would care to walk with me tonight, or will you be taking a carriage?"

"Oh, I…I believe Pascal and I will be arriving a bit later."

"I see." Josef turns to leave but struggles to take his gaze off her. "I will see you there, then."

At the sound of the door closing, Pascal comes out from behind the screen. He gently wraps his arms around Anna and presses his lips to her neck. He senses she is not entirely present. "We can go early, if you like."

She reaches back and touches his bare hip, then moves her hand over. "No. Tell me more about this book."

"Shall we begin with the position of the antelope, the boa, or the tiger?" He turns her to face him.

"Those all sound absolutely *beastly*."

Josef and Christoph arrive at Count Meusberger's mansion separately, Josef on foot, Christoph by carriage. Klara arrives shortly after, accompanied by Herr Weisman. The duke's confidant watches the room, keeping attention on the clockmaker and the duchess. Josef and Klara maintain decorum and discretion by staying on opposite sides of Meusberger's grand ballroom. They hardly look at one another from across the way.

The masquerade masks are as unique as each individual in attendance: devils and harlequins, animals and lovers. The fashion is of elegant opulence. The clockmaker and doctor look particularly refined in their ruffled shirts, embroidered vests, and brocaded jackets. Even their shoe buckles have an extra shine. The orchestra plays each hand-selected piece to perfection. No detail is over-looked.

A half hour into the evening, Count Meusberger makes his way to the floor. He attempts to greet each of his guests individually. When he reaches Josef and Christoph, he kisses the cheeks of each of them, then takes the clockmaker's hand.

"This evening would not be possible without you, Herr Kronecker."

"You're very kind," Josef replies, "though exaggerating."

"I am honest as well as grateful. There is nothing exaggerated. I've been practicing the allemande relentlessly, by the way."

"I can imagine."

"Tonight, I will partake like a young man bursting of passion and vigor—for dancing, that is."

"We can only hope."

The count laughs like no one else. "Now, have either of you seen the Duke and Duchess Brunner?"

"The duchess, I last saw over that way." Christoph points. "The duke, however, is at home, convalescing."

"Pity…No matter. It is the duchess I most wish to see. She was the inspiration for this lovely event, you know."

"Inspiration?" Josef says.

"It was her idea, really. 'Salzburg needs a night out,' she said. So, I obliged. Please excuse me." The count hurries off with an unnatural lightness in his step.

Christoph watches with great interest. "What alterations, exactly, did you make to his legs?"

"Mostly in the nature of springs. There's a fair amount of hopping and skipping in the allemande. Why?"

"Curious."

Josef searches the room.

"She's over near the orchestra," Christoph says.

"I was looking for Anna. She said she would be late, but I thought she'd be here by now."

It isn't long before the count presents himself at the center of the dance floor with his chosen partner, a lovely young lady of ample panniers, wig, and bosom— the first of several companions of his for the evening, actually; all of whom are amply endowed, for that is the count's preference.

The orchestra begins, appropriately, with the music of André Campra. From its first lively step, one can see what separates the allemande from the gavotte or the subdued minuet. The allemande is about hand-holding, the intertwining of fingers, and the intermingling of arms and bodies with spinning rosettes, all done with distinctive hopping and elegant sweeps of the legs.

From the count's first dance step, Josef understands what prompted Christoph's earlier curiosity. Meusberger moves with such agility that he would be the envy of any ballerina, and there's an uncharacteristic, even unnatural, strength to his hops. Guests marvel at the corpulent count's grace. *Ohs* and *Ahs* begin to fill the ballroom as the dance progresses.

❂ ❧ ❂ ❧ ❂

Mert Zimic, a man whose misfortune goes beyond just his name. Since birth, poor Zimic knew only orphanages as his home—not one, but several. The first burned down and others ran out of funding. Eventually, he was marked as unadoptable due to his various nervous tendencies: fear of the dark, claustrophobia, and the like. As an adult, his desire to be useful and helpful often allowed him to overcome his nervousness, fortunately. He would act against his nature so that he could do for others. *Un*-fortunately, those "others" were not always the cream of society. Having earned a reputation on the street as someone who could get things done, he'd come to do a fair amount of work for Duke Leopold Brunner—work not always considered reputable or legal but useful…to Brunner. Which is why he now paces in the cold and dark at the front of Kronecker's Timepieces. He croons a children's song—something he does to quell his anxieties.

"Now Tom with his pipe made such a noise," he sings, "that he pleased both the girls and boys…" His breath freezing hangs about him. "And they all stopped to hear him play…"

He waits for a colleague. Felix Schicklgruber. Considering what is known of Zimic, the kind of man who would associate with him is exactly who Herr Schicklgruber is.

"…Over the Hills and Far Away," Zimic sings.

Schicklgruber finally arrives, and Mert promptly gives him a smack across the head. "You're late."

"I got lost. You're terrible at directions," Felix snaps.

"Maybe if you could read."

Felix looks into the shop's window. "We're going to steal a clock?"

"No. We're just going to have ourselves a look

around." Zimic jimmies the lock and opens the door.

"For what?"

"Information," Zimic says as they enter. "Something that might be suspicious, incriminating, or otherwise useful."

Felix stays close to his cohort. He admires the craftmanship around him. "Could I help myself to a clock before we leave?"

"No."

With a disgruntled spit, Felix proceeds through the dark display aisles, then stops and asks, "No one is here?"

"No one. Why?"

"Thought I heard something."

The two quietly wait and listen. Satisfied they are alone, Zimic says, "You look around the upstairs. I'll stay down here."

They separate. Felix stops on occasion to gander at a clock or listen for a noise he thought he heard.

No stranger to this type of work, Zimic knows that secrets, especially useful ones, lie beyond the surface—on the other side of doors or behind curtains, one of which he discovers soon in his search. Lit candle in hand, he takes a deep, calming breath before drawing back the black drape to the workroom. He sings his happy tune in a jittery whisper and peers into the eerie glow of candlelight.

"Tom he was a piper's son…"

Nothing nefarious about worktables and tools.

"He learned to play when he was young…"

The shelves and bins of clock parts offer little more.

"But the only tune that he could play…"

But there's a door.

"Was 'Over the Hills and Far Away'…"

That leads to another door that emanates a god-awful odor.

Zimic stops at the undefinable noises coming from behind the second door. He looks about in hopes Felix has joined him, but no such luck. With a step forward, he sings again, a little louder:

"Now Tom with his pipe made such a noise…"

There comes a sound of squeaking.

"That he pleased both the girls and boys…"

And scratching.

"And they all stopped to hear him play…"

He reaches out a shaking hand. Takes the knob. Waits.

"'Over the Hills…"

He opens the door.

"'…and Far Awaauuugh!'"

Galileo bolts from the room.

Zimic falls to his ass. The candle slips from his hand, scalding a finger on its way to the floor. As he reaches for it, Galileo head-butts his hand. Zimic jerks his arms back. He lifts the light in the direction the fat cat's purring. His tongue creeps to the back of his throat at the sight of the steel of the feline's hindquarters.

"M-Mercy," he says, choking on the words.

There is movement beyond the open door. Ramses the rat, his wheels squeaking, scurries past. Zimic yelps. He wants to look farther into the next room but can't move. Strange smells waft over him. Glowing eyes stare back at him. He hears a child-like whine, only to realize it comes from him. He tosses the candle through the menagerie's doorway. His eyes widen. Illuminated in the uneven light is the wingless Annabel, hopping to and fro. Her head tilts from one side to the other, scrutinizing the odd, trembling fellow on the floor. She caws.

Zimic screams. Faster than a scampering rat, he is on his feet and in a run. In the dark, the poor, agitated criminal stumbles in one direction, then another. His desperate search for the way out careens him into tables and shelves. He trips over something heavy and falls to the floor.

His voice quivers. He reaches out and takes hold of…something. He feels soft cloth and lace. And…arms? Squeezing them, he moves his own fingers down to what seem to be small hands. He reaches up, fighting the weight of trepidation, and touches a solid, head-shaped object. Zimic's vision adjusts to the dark. With the help of a moonbeam filtering through the skylight above, he makes contact with a pair of shimmering eyes—open and staring.

They blink.

Terror strangles him. Not a sound manages to come from Zimic's throat, but he finds he can still run. He rips from the room, nearly tearing down the black curtain on his way. Tears blur his sight as he tries any and every door in hopes one will lead him outside.

He finds a sitting room. A study. Then a room

with a fire burning in the hearth. A pair of upright steel legs beside a bed. A man and woman. He wipes his eyes and brings into focus the intertwining of bodies and flesh. Where does one end and the other begin?

It is the last sight Mert Zimic can take.

Felix, having hurried down from upstairs, arrives in time to watch his friend drop to floor in the doorway of Anna's room. The two lovers stare with mouths agape as the would-be thief runs from the shop, abandoning his accomplice and forgetting to steal a clock on the way.

⊕   ૨   ⊕   ૨   ⊕

The music has stopped in Count Meusberger's ballroom. The dancers have cleared the floor—all but one, that is. The count himself remains, lying there in an agonized heap with Dr. Baeder kneeling by his side.

Just moments before, Josef, Christoph, and everyone else marveled as the count bounded into the air, only to land with a gruesome crack from his mid-section and a painful shriek from his throat. The sturdy frame-work around his legs did not allow him to fall. Instead, Count Meusberger's torso slipped and hung downward like a string-less marionette as he cried for help. Josef and a few other gentlemen helped the count to a prone position on the floor. Then, without forethought, Christoph removed Meusberger's pantaloons for a closer examination.

Now all marvel in silence at the gleaming steel wrapping the count's legs. Everyone, that is, but Duchess Brunner. Before the unfortunate accident, while the others were enraptured by their host's dancing abilities, Klara whispered to Herr Weisman, "Enough of distractions. It is time for action," then exited the mansion to her awaiting carriage.

"We need to move him," Christoph says as the count emits distressful whines. "Someplace more comfortable than this floor."

Servants direct the men to a large sitting room. Josef takes the count's feet, while the others manage the rest of Meusberger's squirming girth. His thoughts whirl with concern about what all of Salzburg will be talking about the next day: the count's condition and his appendages of steel.

He finds himself also thinking of Anna and whatever might have kept her from Meusberger's ball.

A second after Zimic's collapse, Pascal sprang from the bed like a cat and lifted Anna from him to her perch upon the steel limbs. Then he started after Felix.

"No, Pascal," Anna told him.

He stopped, nearly tripping over Zimic in the process. She rushed to kneel beside the motionless criminal.

"He's dead," she said.

"I thought he just fainted!"

"No, no, no. Oh, my God. He's dead."

"What do we do?"

Anna collected her thoughts. "You need to go get Dr. Baeder. And Josef. Run."

Pascal turned.

"Wait," she snapped. "Put on some clothes."

He hurried back into the room, dressed, and then tore from the shop as fast as he could, leaving Anna to deal with escaped, scurrying critters.

Pascal arrives at Count Wilhelm Meusberger's mansion

disheveled, winded, and damp with sweat. He doesn't give the servants who don't recognize him a chance to deny him entry. He pushes past them and cuts through the crowd of guests in search of the doctor and the clockmaker. He finds Josef first.

"Pascal? What has happened?"

"I don't know exactly." Pascal gasps for air. "I need to find Dr. Baeder. You must come back to the shop. There's a body."

"A body?"

"Where is Dr. Baeder?"

Josef leads him to the sitting room, where Christoph has been examining the count, who lies on a chaise lounge. At the sight of them, Meusberger beams through pangs of discomfort. "Maestro Künzi? How wonderful of you to come. Pardon me for not rising to properly welcome you."

Christoph turns to Josef. "I believe he may have broken his hip. We need to take him to the hospital without haste." He then takes in the unexpected, rumpled presence of Pascal. "What has happened?"

From a corner of the ballroom, Matthew Weisman finally sees something of interest: Herr

Kronecker, Dr. Baeder, and the bedraggled pianist departing with a clear sense of urgency.

❂ ❧ ❂ ❧ ❂

Felix Schicklgruber's eyes burn and water in the smoky tavern where he now sits. In front of him, there's a stein of ale. On either side of him sits one of his comrades in thievery. They hunker next to him, their attention fully baited on his tale of that evening's incident.

"Go on, Felix," one of them prods.

"What happened to Mert?" the other asks.

Now Felix's eyes burn from the image he will take to his grave. He rubs them in hopes of erasing it, but the terrible embers remain. "He dropped there as lifeless as a still-born calf."

The other two gulp and lean closer. "W-What happened?"

Felix closes his eyes. "Oh, it was out-right horrific. The pair of them were on the bed."

"Go on."

"She was on top of him, her head between his legs." Felix takes a shaky drink of his ale. With a howl, he drops his head into his hands. "They were *cannibals!*

Oh, my dear Christ, he had eaten off her legs. She had devoured his hand. And…and she was starting on his…John Thomas."

Felix's friends look at each other with horror and then at their pitiful companion with concern.

"Her legs were gone I tell you!" Felix buries his face into his crossed arms upon the table.

Both men place a comforting hand on Felix's shoulders, wide-eyed, then shake their heads at one another.

⊕ ❧ ⊕ ❧ ⊕

Anna, sans clothing, successfully collects Galileo and Ramses after chasing them about the shop. She then shoos Annabel into the back room. "I'm lucky you don't have wings, you stupid bird."

"Caw."

She hears a sound coming from Josef's study. With Galileo tucked under her right arm and Ramses squirming in her left hand, Anna stands at the black curtain. When the sound doesn't repeat, she turns, sensing a presence. There, she sees Klara.

"Oh…my," is all the duchess can say at the sight

of Anna.

"Duchess? What are you——?"

"Oh, dear girl. I never imagined. You poor, dear woman."

Anna waves away the duchess's surprise. "Madam, I need your help. There's a dead man in my room."

"What? Pascal?"

"No, not Pascal. I don't know who the man is or what he's doing here."

Klara hurries to find the body of Zimic lying on the floor. She recognizes him in the dim glow of firelight.

"Do you know who he is?" Anna asks from behind her.

"No, of course not. Some vagrant, I imagine. What happened?"

Anna relates the events of the past half hour.

"Caw." Annabel hops from the back room.

Then Galileo decides he's been restrained long enough and squirms from Anna's hold. The action brings her right hand and legs to Klara's attention once more, as well as the fact she is unclothed.

"Annamarie," she says like a mother to a child, "we must get you covered. Have you a chemise or something?"

Anna gestures to an armoire behind the piano. Klara crosses to it and returns with a white linen nightgown. She lifts it up to Anna's head, but pauses.

"Dear, put down the rat."

"But…"

"That vile thing is the least of our worries right now."

Anna pouts but sets Ramses gently on the floor. "Ramses is not vile."

The duchess dresses her. "You named the thing?"

"Yes—well, Josef did. Ramses has been here longer than I have."

"I don't think I'll ever understand the two of you. You're meant for each other, that's for sure." Klara straightens the gown, helping it to drape Anna's slender figure. "I can see why you'd want to strum a young man like Herr Künzi, but once the novelty has worn off, you might want to reconsider your options." Klara gives Anna a once-over. "This doesn't quite cover your…um…legs, does it?"

"I don't usually wear them to bed," Anna says with an awkward laugh.

"No." Klara smiles faintly, "I suppose you wouldn't." She reaches a hand to Anna's. "What happened to you, dear? I just can't imagine how a woman could end up like this."

You haven't seen much of the world, then, have you? Anna considers saying. But instead, she says, "I have some leggings I wear. It makes them appear natural, in the right light."

Anna finds them at her bedside.

"Let me help," Klara says. "I have a feeling we're going to have company soon."

For a moment, Anna felt almost calm, but now she worries again. "What makes you say that?"

The duchess looks at the dead Zimic. "Just a feeling."

Her feeling proves correct. Before she can get the leggings on Anna, Josef's voice booms from the dark of the shop. "What the hell?"

Pascal appears, leaping over Zimic in a rush to embrace Anna.

Christoph kneels down and examines the body.

Ramses the rat sniffs it.

"Meow, purr," says Galileo, circling before the warm embers in the fireplace.

"Caw," adds Annabel.

From behind the men, standing deeper in the shadows, Herr Weisman says, "Yes. *Hell* indeed."

FOURTEEN

Of

MAD MEN AND WOMEN

Dawn comes with a predominance of gray. Not the hue of stone, but the blue and black misty tones of morning still clinging to night. Anna and Pascal lie close to one another. He sleeps; she remains awake. Her back presses against his chest and stomach. She feels the motion of his breathing, and the warmth of his breath on her neck. She relishes the weight of his leg upon her hip, the way it stretches downward from her as though it were her own missing limb. It brings comfort to her troubling thoughts.

Anna had always found something suspect about Klara. Now her doubts are tenfold. What was the duchess doing in the shop? She touches the end of her right arm to Pascal's thigh. *Is he really just a novelty?* She wonders how the duchess could so casually encourage her to consider Josef for a lover instead.

Josef.

He was taken away only hours ago. A pair of the duke's men had arrived on the heels of Herr Weisman. Witness to Anna's physical state, the escaped menagerie, and especially Zimic's lifeless body, Weisman promptly had the clockmaker arrested.

Now the clockmaker lies alone in a gray room within the bowels of the Brunner's palace, suffering his own sleeplessness. The only respite from his anger and fear is the consolation that he was not thrown in an actual prison. He looks about the dismal, locked room and gives a sardonic chuckle. "It could be worse," he mutters, wishing Christoph was there to appreciate the morose humor.

An hour later, his wish comes true. Josef sits upright at the sound of the door's lock turning. There's a pause before it opens, and in walks Christoph. The door is closed and locked behind him.

"I'm so sorry, Josef."

Josef stands, firmly taking his friend's hand. "You have nothing to be sorry about."

"I should have anticipated this lunacy."

"Who could have predicted?" He motions for

Christoph to take the room's only chair as he sits on the edge of the bed.

Christoph looks down at his feet. "Not but a week ago, Brunner tried to coerce me into replacing his heart with yours."

"But I'm using it. I'm quite attached to it, actually."

"He didn't care. He's running out of time. He's desperate."

"You talked him out of it, I presume."

Christoph gives an unconvincing shrug.

"What an absurd idea. My heart won't accommodate his size. He'd be able to do little more than sit around like an invalid."

"I think he would rather be invalid than dead. Many a great man has ruled from a chair."

"It would take a great man to rule from a chair. Leopold Brunner is not that man." Josef sinks at Christoph's downtrodden face. "How could you have known this madman was so mad?"

There is a cough and the shuffling of feet on the other side of the door. The two friends shake their heads.

"It seems we have ears upon us," Christoph says.

Josef shouts at the door: "Could someone bring us some tea and hot chocolate?" He grins. "So you think that's what this is all about? He wants my heart?"

"I can't suspect otherwise."

Josef sighs. "How is Count Meusberger, by the way?"

"Resting. He'll be confined to bed for some time. Who knows if he'll dance again. Walking may be hard enough, even with assistance from you."

Josef hangs his head.

Christoph looks about the room, taking in its somber splendor. "It could be worse."

They laugh.

◉ ❧ ◉ ❧ ◉

Josef sits before Bishop von Bohn in a room larger yet equally uninviting as the one in which he spent the night. The bishop sits behind a dark wood table much bigger than one man should ever need to conduct any sort of business. The two eye each other like chess players in a critical match. Josef waits patiently for His Excellency to speak, as it's clearly the bishop's move.

"I wanted a moment to speak with you privately, before my brother comes in," von Bohn says. "I hope you don't mind."

"Have I another choice?"

The bishop offers an apologetic smile. "Have you read La Mettrie's *L'homme Machine?*"

"Wasn't he persecuted by the Church, and all copies burned?"

"Well," the bishop says with a wry grin, "not all copies. I have one in my library. For research purposes. I ask you as one intellect to another. No persecution."

The clockmaker weighs his answer. "Yes. I've read it."

"Do you agree with La Mettrie? That man is a machine without a soul?"

"La Mettrie did not propose that man has no soul, but that the soul signifies the part of us that thinks."

Von Bohn nods.

"What matters is what *you* think of his view of nature as a mechanism."

"I'm immensely fascinated."

Josef gives a curious glare.

"Serving God was never my idea," the bishop

says. "I always felt I had the soul of a scientist. It was my father who chose this life for me, while grooming Leopold for other things. Out of spite, I even changed my name."

Josef leans forward, giving the bishop his full attention.

"I was quite resentful in my younger years; however, I think I excelled in my seminary studies *because* of my scientific leanings. Now, I've come to find myself with a unique intellectual perspective. My separate paths have converged, so to speak, in these later years. To my delight, I might add."

"This is an invigorating topic of conversation." Josef sits back. "One that I would have welcomed in the comfort of my own sitting room, after a warm meal. It wasn't necessary to confine me against my will."

Again, the bishop smiles an apology.

"Why exactly am I here, Your Excellency?"

"My brother is under the disillusioned impression that he can live forever. Or, at least, much longer than normally expected."

"*Delusional* impression is more appropriate, I think. He must know a new heart will only give him a few more years. I suppose decades, maybe, if he is so fortunate.”

A grave light crosses von Bohn’s face. “Are you familiar with Claude-Nicolas Le Cat, the surgeon?”

“Not personally.”

“It seems he once considered building a mechanical man within which blood could flow, with lungs made of leather that actually filled with air and exhaled. The man would have even secreted fluids from glands made of brass. All to simulate a human body for surgical experiments and education, of course.”

“Of course.”

“A dim reflection of the work you’ve accomplished, don’t you think, Josef?”

“You flatter me.”

“No, I understate, but I also remain pragmatic.” The bishop takes in a deep breath—one of concern. “My brother, however, is not so realistic. He imagines, with greatly misaligned voracity, that such a form could be created, by you, which he could then inhabit. Eternally.”

“I have no doubt I could create such a mechanism, but I could no more put a soul into it than I could turn lead into gold. That kind of magic is a bit beyond my expertise."

"As you said," von Bohn grins, "my brother is—"

The door opens, and the two men are joined by others: Duke Brunner, pushed in a wheeled chair by Elias Dorn, and Herr Weisman. For a lengthy moment, the room is filled with only the squeak of the duke's wheels. The bishop rises and moves so that his brother may take his place behind the table. Two of the duke's men enter. Between them, they carry both sets of Anna's legs, her right hand, and Joop.

Josef stands. One of the men gestures for him to stay where he is. They place the appendages and the mechanical boy upon the table, unconcerned that he tips to one side, threatening to fall to the floor.

"You seem concerned, Herr Kronecker," Brunner says. "It's just a toy, is it not?"

"He is a complicated, intricately engineered figurine." Josef attempts to keep his voice level. "I'd appreciate it if he were handled with greater care."

"What does it do?"

"Almost anything a young boy can do: walk, dance, play."

"Sounds like a toy to me." The duke leans close

to Joop. "But could you demonstrate?"

"I cannot. He requires a disc to direct him what to do."

"I don't understand."

"To put it in the most simplistic terms, he resembles a highly sophisticated music box, but instead of playing a tune, he replicates human motion. There are different discs for different actions."

Brunner looks to Elias. "Where are these discs? Did you not bring them?"

The priest responds with a bewildered stare.

"When we are done here, I want you to fetch me those discs."

Elias bows his head and takes a seat at the far end of the table.

The bishop moves to look closer at Joop with a fascinated gleam in his eye. He circles to the front of the table. "May I touch it?"

Josef gives a wary nod as he sits back down.

Von Bohn gently prods the boy, feeling his arms and legs. "This is where the disc goes?" He points to the slot in the back.

Josef nods.

He inspects Joop's hands and face. "The detail is extraordinary. But I don't see a winding mechanism. How does he work?"

"He is self-perpetual," Josef answers. "When activated, his movement winds his springs. He functions by a constant cycle of storing and using energy."

"Amazing," the bishop says.

"So, he could run forever. Eternally," the duke concludes.

"In theory. He could surely outlive us all."

"Then you think of it as a living being. Do you believe it has a soul? An immortal self?" asks the duke.

"Metaphorically. I believe he is as alive as anyone in this room. We are human beings. He is a mechanical being. We have the mental qualities of reason, emotion, memory, consciousness—a soul, as you say. Joop's soul is within his discs, directing him what do and how to act."

"Why do you keep calling it 'he'?" Elias asks.

Ignoring the impetuous priest, Brunner continues, "You contend we have no free will, then."

"On the contrary," says Josef. "Our will is free, but we choose not to wield it as such. It's easier that way. Blissful as sheep we are.”

“And what of your assistant’s legs?”

“What of them?”

“Are they living?”

“Of course not. They’re tools—instruments that allow her a quality of life she would not otherwise have.”

“Don’t you think your ideals are a bit confused?”

“They are as clear to me as crystal.”

While the duke and clockmaker engage in conversation, Bishop von Bohn examines the sets of legs and the hand with restrained interest. “These belonged to Annamarie?” he eventually asks.

“They still belong to her, I hope,” Josef replies. “She can’t get along very well without them. But, yes, they are hers. With these, she resumed a useful place in society with a modicum of dignity.”

Bishop von Bohn’s posture melts with heartbroken sympathy. “That dear girl. I never knew.”

“That was the intention.”

The bishop further scrutinizes the legs. “This set here seems more sophisticated than the other. A greater variety of springs, some the likes I’ve never seen. A system for balance, too, I believe.”

"Your Excellency is very perceptive. The second pair allows her greater mobility over irregular terrain. She can even climb stairs."

"Remarkable."

Brunner grows impatient. "For what purpose did you build this boy? I'm sure it wasn't on a whim. What was your intention?"

Josef weighs his response carefully. "Joop has been my drawing board, you might say. From him, other mechanicals have come about. Thus, his name."

"*God will multiply*," clarifies the bishop.

"*Golem* would have been more fitting," Elias says. Then, with a sudden look of horror, he thrusts his hand out and pushes Joop from the table.

Josef stands. "Be careful, you oaf."

"He *moved*." Elias gasps. "He looked at me. I—"

The duke laughs until he coughs, painfully. "Perhaps, Father, it is *your* veracity that should be questioned." he manages to say. Catching his breath, he turns back to Josef. "So, you are God now?"

"Not at all. God created me. I'm just passing it on."

"And what other devices have you made, thanks

to this…Joop? Legs for Count Meusberger, I've been told. Anything else?"

"Merely trifles. Experiments in themselves."

"You consider your own heart a trifle?"

"So that's what this inquisition is about."

"This is no inquisition," Brunner tells him. "There is no torture."

Josef looks to Joop slumped on floor. "I'll be the judge of that."

"May we see it?" von Bohn asks as pleasantly as he can. "Your heart?"

Knowing the futility of refusing and out of respect for the bishop, Josef opens his vest, his shirt, and then peels the "skin" from his chest. Von Bohn steps in and bends toward Josef, and Herr Weisman pushes the duke closer. Through the heart's glass casing, the gears can be seen turning and the rods can be seen pumping. In the men's faces are all the descriptive words Josef has heard before: amazing, magnifique, *miraculous.*

From behind the bishop, Elias says, "How do you love, then?"

Both von Bohn and Josef laugh at the naïve priest with such scornful condemnation that Elias promptly cowers. The duke motions for Weisman to move him back behind the table. Once settled, he asks, "And what of the murdered man found in your shop?"

"Murdered?" Josef exclaims. "That thief—whoever he was—was dead when I returned from Count Meusberger's. I've been told he merely dropped dead from who-knows-what."

"As you say."

Josef puts his chest back together and closes his shirt and vest. "You're right. This is no inquisition, nor a trial, but a sentencing."

"I'm a patient man, Josef." Brunner attempts to sit as royally as he can. "Until I'm not any longer. I want—no, I *need* your heart. Your heart for your innocence. Otherwise, you'll be found guilty of a heinous crime. Give me your heart, and then you can make yourself another at your leisure."

Josef steps forward with as much of a respectful, imploring posture as he can manage. "I'm telling you, sir, you can't have it. What I mean is, my heart is practically worthless to you. It's too small to serve you properly. You would be able to do little more than lie in bed or sit in a chair. Any greater activity would overtax the mechanics. You would soon find yourself in this very same circumstance."

The duke crosses his arms.

Josef continues, "I have completed *your* heart. Just this evening. A few final tests, and it will be ready for you. One day, two at the most. You only need allow me to get back to my shop. The sooner you do, the sooner you can begin the rest of what could be a very long life."

Brunner remains still.

"I also ask that my assistant's legs and hand be returned to her. She's suffered enough difficulties. Those devices allow her some shred of dignity."

Brunner shakes his head. "You'll return to your room while I give this deliberation." With a wave of his hand, he orders his men to lead Josef from the room.

As soon as the clockmaker is gone, the bishop steps forward. "Please, brother, consider Herr Kronecker's requests as an act of good faith. If you wish, I will personally escort him back to his shop and ensure he gives your heart his exclusive attention."

A smirk curls the duke's mouth. "If I agree, I will keep Joop here with me. Perhaps we can get to know each other a little better.”

🕐 ❧ 🕑 ❧ 🕒

Anna tends the menagerie without her legs and hand. She wears a shirt of Pascal's that covers her body just enough without encumbering her movement, which consists of dragging herself across the floor and pulling herself up to rest on stools or tables. The critters stare with great interest at the familiar yet strange attendant before them. Her muscles are unacquainted with the method in which she moves and works, and Anna's arms ache, yet she does not cry; she does not curse.

Glancing over her shoulder, she sees Pascal enter the space and attempts to ignore his pitying expression. “I'll need to attach handles to tables and counters throughout the shop to help me climb,” she tells him.

“I can assist you.”

“I'll not be a burden.”

“It's no burden.” He reaches to take her.

“*No*,” she snaps. “You can help by letting me do for myself. Don't you have a performance coming up? Shouldn't you be preparing?”

“I've considered canceling it. Until you have your

legs back.”

Anna drops down from a stool, then proceeds to push a food bowl along the floor with the end of her left arm. “I’ll never have my legs back.”

“You know what I mean.”

“All too well.” She strokes Galileo’s head. “Now, go prepare for your concert. I’ll manage fine without you.”

“Anna, I love—”

“Don’t ever put me above your music. Or you’ll no longer have me.”

Pascal hovers, bewildered and unsure.

“Please…go.”

The pianist takes a deep breath and pulls his shoulders back. He knows she’s right. She can manage without him, and he must play his music. Nonetheless, turning his back and leaving her there on the floor is the hardest thing he’s ever done.

✦ ☙ ✦ ☙ ✦

Josef sits again in the small gray room awaiting the duke’s decision. *Better than in a cell awaiting to be hanged,* he considers. He finds the silence disconcerting. It magnifies every small noise.

Like the creak of a stair down the hall.

The shuffle of feet outside the room.

A scratch at the locked door. Followed by another.

It seems the duke is not the only large rodent living here, crosses the clockmaker's mind. "Hello?" he says.

One more scratch, punctuated by the sound of something slumping against the door. More footsteps descend the stairs and approach his room, followed by voices Josef thinks belong to the pair of the duke's men from earlier.

"How the hell did that get here?" asks one.

"We better get him back upstairs before anyone notices," says the other. "I don't want to have to explain this."

"You called it 'him.'"

"Well…he looks so real."

Josef steps to the door and listens as the collective footsteps return to the stairs and then upward. Then the silence resumes.

Brunner sits alone with Joop, he in his wheeled chair, the clockwork lad propped up on a Chippendale. Brunner watches with great anticipation for Joop to do…something? He wheels himself closer and reaches out to give the boy a poke. Then he nudges him in the shoulder, but Joop remains motionless.

"I suppose we'll have to wait for those discs of yours, after all." Brunner sighs. He wheels himself to the door. Before leaving, he scrutinizes the boy one more time. "No matter. You've given me hope, young man."

⊕ ❧ ⊕ ❧ ⊕

Anna hears someone enter the shop. With impatient determination, she drags herself from the back. "Pascal, I told you—"

She stops at the sight of Bishop von Bohn and Elias Dorn. They, too, stop at the sight of her, there on the floor like a broken glass figurine. The priest looks upon her with repulsion rather than pity, but the bishop holds back a tear. He wants to comfort her, assure her. Instead, he honors her dignity with a smile and tells her, "I thought you could use these."

Two of the duke's men carry in a set of her legs

Of Gilded Flesh / 306

and her hand.

It is all Anna can do to compose herself at the bishop's kindness. Propped unsteadily with her left hand, she manages a grateful bow of her head. "Thank you, Your Excellency." She motions to her room with her handless wrist and tells the men, "Place them in there, next to the bed."

They heft the appendages.

Bishop von Bohn says, "My brother wouldn't approve if he knew I've brought the most recent version of your legs. But then, he wouldn't be able to tell the difference."

Anna gives a dim smile, then frowns. "Where is Joop?"

"It was a compromise. He wants to examine him. Which means he'll stare at him for a while, give him a poke or two, and be done."

Anna acknowledges Elias's presence with a scornful glare when the priest clears his throat. "I've come for the box of discs," he says. "Those that control the mechanical boy."

Anna looks to the bishop.

"I assure you Joop and the discs will be returned

as soon as the duke loses interest."

Elias turns on the bishop. "That was never—"

"They're in the workroom," Anna says, "on an upper shelf."

The priest skirts around her as though she were a plague-infested heap, leaving Anna and von Bohn alone.

"Where is Josef?" she asks.

"He has gone to his study to work."

Anna finally notices the faint glow of candlelight from beneath the closed study door. "Of course he has." She chuckles, a bit embarrassed. "I didn't hear him come in."

The duke's men return and take a place on either side of the study door. Elias comes from the workroom with the box of discs under one arm.

"Go ahead. I'll follow shortly," the bishop tells him, and the priest happily removes himself from the shop. "The duke has given Josef twenty-four hours to finish his heart. Dr. Baeder is beginning preparations for the surgery. Two, actually, if necessary."

Anna's eyes open wide with comprehension.

Bishop von Bohn steps closer and goes down on one knee before her. He takes her hand. "Let's pray it won't come to that. Have faith that he will finish his work successfully." He rises. "He's not to be disturbed, Annamarie. I'll come back in a few hours to see how he's progressed."

As soon as the bishop is gone, Anna pulls herself toward the study. One of the men puts out a hand for her to stop. "Josef!" she calls out.

The door opens. The clockmaker peers out— three feet above Anna's head. Then he looks down, and his hunched, tired body hunches even farther. "My dear, I'm so sorry."

"What can I do, Josef?"

"The bishop and I got you your legs back."

"Yes. I saw. Thank you. But how can I help you?"

"You can leave me to work. It shouldn't be long." He starts to close the door.

"Shall I bring you some chocolate?"

"No. Thank you, though." And with that, he closes and locks the door.

It's nearly dawn as Elias hurries along the quiet streets back to Duke Brunner's palace. For the priest, it's a little too quiet. Just as he never looks forward to his daily meditations because he doesn't find solace in the sound of his own breathing, Elias now wishes there were more to hear than the echo of his footsteps.

Wait. Echo?

Elias stops and turns, unsure if he's hearing a reverberation of his own steps or footfalls belonging to someone else. The shadows of morning reveal nothing, and he continues on. The extra pair of steps returns. Elias stops again in hopes of surprising his follower.

"Hello? Good morning?" he queries the silence.

When no response comes, the priest rounds a corner and brings into view St. Peter's Cathedral. He smiles. Light from an upper window urges Elias toward the front steps. Surely there must be someone there to speak to, to share salutations with and alleviate the quiet. A framework of scaffolding clings to the side of one tower and that reminds him of how many centuries the structure has stood there, fallen, and been rebuilt. The sound of shuffling feet teases him from across the square.

Elias hurries into the church without looking back. He wants to call out but is restrained by the sacredness of the space. The priest never fails to be amazed and humbled by the immensity of the cathedral's interior. Standing before the baptismal font, he looks up to the muralled dome with reverence, as though he were looking to heaven. Dawn's light seeps through windows and sets aglow the altar's ironwork and wood; it brings to him a deep, comforted sigh.

Elias takes in the baroque details as he begins to wander. He takes a set of stairs up one of the towers. When he reaches a window that leads out to the scaffolding he saw earlier, Elias gazes out at the city awash by the coming day—until his bliss is interrupted by the sound of footsteps once more.

They shuffle below, perhaps circling the baptismal font, with the arrhythmic cadence of someone enjoying the cathedral's beauty. Or someone lost. Or someone looking for something.

There's a pause before the steps continue in the stairwell below.

"Good morning," Elias says to the gray stairwell from which he came.

The steps continue their ascent, clumsily, as though the climb poses a challenge to the climber. Elias wonders if this person is perhaps infirm or elderly. As the darkened form takes shape, he sees that they are neither sick nor old, but small, like a child. Elias leans forward. "Well, hello there."

In a beam of morning light, a youthful head emerges, with silk-like hair and leathery skin. Glistening eyes of moonstone look up and meet the priest's now widening stare.

Elias steps back. "No. It c-can't be."

A pair of small hands thrusts forward and snatches away the box of discs from beneath the priest's arm. Elias attempts to distance himself, backing away to the scaffolding outside the window behind him. His breaths are pulsating, irregular, and sharp. His attention is so fixated on the boy's face and the silence from his gaping mouth that Elias fails to watch where he steps. His foot misses the scaffold's platform, and the railing gives way under the weight of the imbalanced priest.

◷ 🐌 ◷ 🐌 ◷

Josef leans over his worktable and stares down at a box, wherein lies the duke's heart. He opens it and removes the device. He studies it, refers to his notes. He looks back at Duke Brunner's future there in his hands.

Of Gilded Flesh / 312

The clockmaker's eyes widen. If his own heart could skip a beat, it would.

Something's not right. A part is missing. He examines it closer. A critical gear in the mechanism has been removed—no, *ripped* from its place, and other parts within have been left mangled in the process. Josef looks about his workspace for other evidence of damage. He falls to his knees to search the floor. In the dim light, he spies, behind his desk, a portrait of a woman; her exquisite eyes stare back at him.

Josef's head burns. A gut-wrenching epiphany moves him from underneath the worktable to his armchair, where he collapses, every fiber of his will shattered. He'd been so stupid. *Nothing more than her pawn.* It could take weeks to repair this damage. *Oh, how very, very stupid…*

The now worthless heart drops from Josef's hand to the floor with an anticlimactic thump. His body sinks farther into the armchair, becoming nothing more than an empty, motionless heap. He would shout, cry, or beat his fists on the table, but all that requires too much energy, too much emotion—and he has neither of which left in him.

FIFTEEN

Of

DYING

The clockmaker goes under the doctor's scalpel once more. This time, though, the duke lies on a gurney next to him.

Christoph had never actually considered switching their hearts; he had intended all along to give Leopold Brunner Josef's older, malfunctioning cardiac device, expecting it to fail shortly after the procedure. However, the duke—being much more experienced at malfeasance—anticipated the possibility of the ruse.

"I'll have men watching you closely during this operation, Herr Doctor," Brunner told Christoph before the surgery. "Just in case you decide your friendship is worth more to you than your profession—or your life."

Josef experiences yet another transplant with success—if you can call a barely conscious state of recuperation a success. He survives but remains nearly comatose after the procedure.

Across the city, Anna agonizes over what she could be doing to help.

"He should be here at home," she tells Christoph. "He recovered so well last time, and I'm better able to care for him now."

"I don't disagree, but I'm afraid to move him. His old heart is working, but not well. On the occasions he's awake, he's barley coherent. He hallucinates. He babbles. His life hangs too precariously between dream and death right now."

"All the more reason he should be here."

Christoph shakes his head. "Let's see what the next few days bring."

What they bring are moments of growing clarity from the clockmaker, and hope for Christoph. Apprehensive hope, but hope nonetheless. During one of the doctor's rounds, Josef tells him, "I saw Joop last night."

"What's that?" Christoph examines his friend. "You dreamt of Joop?"

"No. He was here. I woke to the presence of someone near me and there he was."

"Hallucinations are common with laudanum."

"It was very real."

"Oh? What was he doing?"

"Nothing. He just sat there and kept me company. It was nice to have a visitor."

"What do you mean? I visit you quite often."

"A visitor who doesn't constantly prod me, I mean."

"I prod because I care."

Josef laughs, then cringes.

"How's your pain, Josef? I could increase the dosage if need be."

"No, I would rather ache and be present than feel nothing in a shroud of delirium. The hurt lets me know I'm still with the living."

"It's nice to have you back. But do let me know if it becomes unbearable."

🕐 ❧ 🕑 ❧ 🕒

Josef regrets longing for visitors, because soon, upon waking from a fitful rest, he gets what he asked for. Klara sits at his bedside.

"My dear Josef," she says in that voice he has

come to loathe. She caresses his forehead and kisses his cheek. "I'm so sorry. Leopold was supposed to die before it came to this."

He shakes his head. If he had the strength, the clockmaker would demand she leave. He raises a hand to push her away, but she takes it and holds it tenderly.

"You weren't supposed to be caught in the middle of all this."

"It was you who put me here."

"How can you say that? You must know that I love you."

Josef collects his thoughts, then takes in a deep breath. "I think you love your title more. You always have."

She pulls back, affronted by his blunt tone, and lets his hand drop to the bed.

"I remember"—Josef's eyes water as he searches his foggy memory—"you once said being a duchess was not of your choosing." He strains to sit up. "That is because you would prefer to be a queen, isn't it? Or an empress?"

Klara turns from him.

With an exhausted sigh, he adds, "To think

you've been scheming this all along. From the moment we met."

"That is not true, Josef. When we met, I was only looking for a lover. You were supposed to be a trifle for my amusement. I don't apologize for that. But I felt something for you I hadn't expected. Then I realized the part Anna played in your life. It's she you love. You always have. That is when I saw a different opportunity and concocted this *scheme*, as you call it."

Josef coughs. "Her part? She was raped and mutilated. That was her part."

Klara gives a sad grin. "And to think I was going to give you a painting of myself."

"Please…leave." He closes his eyes.

The duchess watches Josef breathe, thinking he's fallen back to sleep. She leans in close and whispers, "You may be a cynic, but you are also a decent, righteous man. Foolish, but righteous." She kisses his forehead. "I shall try to honor your example. Goodbye, Josef. Whether you survive this or not, goodbye."

Josef is not asleep, and he does hear her. He listens to the door close behind Klara and welcomes the relief that he will never see her again.

Leopold Brunner arrives in Josef's room the following morning. While the clockmaker has struggled with his recovery, the duke's has gone well. It was only a matter of days before he was being rolled about the halls of the hospital in a wheeled chair.

He's pushed to Josef's bedside by Herr Weisman. "You're looking well, Clockmaker."

With a tilt of his head in the duke's direction, Josef replies, "As are you. Are you enjoying my heart?"

"I would have rather had my own, but this will suffice. A small sacrifice, really." Brunner looks to Weisman behind him. "I think I could grow to like this arrangement; although, I may need to acquire a hardier confidant." The duke laughs, and Weisman feigns amusement. "I have complete faith in your recovery, Clockmaker. I expect you to be working in your shop in no time, building yourself yet another new heart." Brunner pauses to be sure he has Josef's attention. "*After* you finish the one you started for me, that is."

Josef sits up. "What are talking about?"

The duke grips the arm of his wheeled chair.

"You didn't think I would be satisfied being confined to one of these for the rest of my life, did you?"

Josef strains to protest, but the faulty mechanism in his chest is unable to keep up with his increased respiratory rate.

Brunner leans forward. "I want *my* heart. I can wait for as long as it takes. I'm in a position to do that now, thanks to you. But I want what's mine. My heart. My reign. My *wife*."

Josef sinks back into his bed with a cough that becomes a laugh.

"Yes. That's the spirit. We'll make history together when you create a whole new body for me to inhabit. Just think of it, Josef."

"Oh, I am thinking of it. Chances are I'll be dead by week's end. This laugh I'm having could be my last, and it is at you."

The duke straightens. "You'd better hope that is not the case. I have kept your macabre partnership with Dr. Baeder from the archbishop for now. But these are precarious times, philosophically speaking. There's still the question of that dead man found in your shop as well. And our poor Elias."

Josef's smile falters.

"You did not hear? The priest was found dead on the steps of St. Peter's. It seems he fell from a great height. Or he was pushed. A rather suspicious turn of events considering everything else, don't you think?"

At the sight of Josef's agitation, Weisman tells the duke, "Sir, I fear he may not make it to the end of the day if we do not leave at this moment."

Brunner nods. With a wave of his hand he directs Weisman to roll him from the room. "Rest well, Herr Kronecker."

The duke is no longer in earshot when Josef mutters, "You better hope you don't have your throat ripped out in the meantime."

⊘   ❧   ⊕   ❧   ⊗

Josef dreams of Joop. He sees them, just him and the mechanical boy, playing together in the shop, hiding-and-seeking with each other among the displays. He swears, in a brief waking moment, that he sees the lad there by his bed in the blurry, flickering candlelight. Josef reaches out a hand, and Joop takes it.

Another time, he dreams of Anna. She is naked

and captivating before him, with human legs and a human hand. They don't make love. Rather, they play backgammon endlessly, in a teasing stalemate, each looking for the dice to roll in their favor.

Josef wakes and looks about his room. "Anna?" he says, but he is alone in the orange candlelight around him.

🕐 ❧ 🕑 ❧ 🕘

Anna can't do enough to distract her worry. She takes a walk and comes upon the flower girl.

"I'm sorry about your priest," the girl calls out.

Anna approaches with a quizzical look.

"I saw him often enter your shop, so I assumed…"

"What of him?"

"Oh, I'm—I'm sorry, ma'am. He was found dead. Outside the church. I thought you'd have heard."

"How? What happened?"

The girl shrugs. "They say he fell down."

"Fell down?"

"From the church."

Expecting to get no more details than that, Anna

wonders if it really matters how he died. She doesn't question whether the news is idle gossip or if it was another clergyman that had been found. She knows in her gut it is true.

"Did you know him well, ma'am?"

"I did. Once," Anna manages.

But not anymore, she thinks, and gives a few coins to the girl before moving on. Any grief she may have for Elias is quashed beneath the weight of greater concerns looming sorrows—the clockmaker, the pianist.

Later, Anna sits with Pascal in Josef's study. He holds her left hand in his right. "You should go see him," he tells her.

"I can't." Her voice is strained and tired from too many nights without sleep. "I fear it will be the last time I see him. It's easier to sit here and remember."

"Is it? When was the last time you saw him?"

"The night of…"

"Yes. We were all in your room. *She* was there, and Josef stood lost and confused beside a dead man. Is that what you want to remember? You want that moment to be your last memory him?"

Anna's throat quivers. "Of course not."

"If this *is* the last time you have to see him—which it may not—you'll regret not taking it."

"I know."

"I'll go with you."

Anna takes a moment, then realizes. "If you don't mind, I'd rather you didn't. I'd prefer to be accompanied by Bishop von Bohn."

Pascal reluctantly agrees that would be best.

Anna cannot bring herself to look at her young lover. She knows the hurt and loss in his gaze would be too much for her to bear right now. Whether Josef survives or not, her and Pascal's time together is nearing its end.

As she always feared: he loves her too much, and she not enough.

⊕ ❧ ⊕ ❧ ⊕

Led by a nurse, Anna and the bishop make their way down a long hall to the clockmaker's room. Von Bohn gives her hand a reassuring squeeze with both of his and tells her he'll wait outside.

Anna stops just inside the door at the sight of

Josef sunken into his bed. His eyes, at first dull and vacant, brighten at seeing her. He mouths, "*Anna.*" She pulls a chair close to his bed and sits.

"You move so elegantly," he says. "No one would think those weren't your own legs."

"But they are my legs. Thanks to you."

"I saw Joop."

Anna leans closer. "He was here?"

Josef nods. "He held my hand."

"I'm sorry I couldn't stop them from taking him."

"What could you have done? He should be home soon. There's no reason for them to keep him."

"Out of spite is reason enough."

Josef lets out a long breath.

Anna takes a cloth from his bedside table and puts it to his damp forehead. "How about you?" she asks. "When are you coming home?"

He looks away. "I can't see if there's a clock in here, but I feel the sun is setting, isn't it?"

"Yes. Nearly."

Turning back to her, his eyes wet, Josef reaches out to Anna with his lithe, weakened fingers and caresses her flawless complexion. She presses against the touch she has so longed for. He feels the heat of her breath upon his hand. "I am so sorry, my dear."

"Sorry for what?"

"For seeing you as nothing but an experiment. I've been so stupid."

A tear rolls down her face and into his palm. "Yes. Yes, you have."

Josef gasps. Anna feels his chest, then opens his gown. Touching his heart, she tells him, "It's slowing. It needs to be wound." She loosens the drawstring of her reticule and removes from it a key.

Josef takes her hand. "Tell me?"

"Anything."

"Did you kill that count? Hirsch?"

"Yes," she says without hesitation.

"How did it feel?"

"I'm not a killer."

"I know that."

"It was an accident."

"But…how did it feel?"

"Wonderful." Anna drops her head as though sitting in a confessional. "Horrible and wonderful."

"He deserved much worse." Josef pushes away

her hand that holds the key. "I don't think I'll be coming home. I think it best if…"

Anna doesn't argue. In a way, she envies him. Oh, how it would feel to sleep forever. She's so often wanted to go on to something better (or nothing—she's never known what to be believe). Yet she hasn't, for the same reason she didn't die on that rocky ravine: the light of life is so very strong in her. Instead, she's kept busy, never allowing thoughts of death to linger. Too busy to die.

Josef Kronecker is an insufferable cynic. He adores hot chocolate, Galileo, and Joop, and even the annoying Annabel. As a self-proclaimed misanthrope, he's also shown himself to be a hypocrite for how much he's done for others. Anna lays her head upon his chest and cries. She lets the tears cleanse her—tears for a good man she loves, who, it turns out, loves her, too.

She cries until she's ready to get on with life, to busy herself again.

Then she inserts the key into his chest and winds his heart.

"I'm not a killer," she tells him. "I'll no more let you die than you allowed me to perish among the rocks."

Josef gives her a woeful yet resigned smile. Anna holds his hand tight as his breathing steadies.

❂ ❧ ❂ ❧ ❂

When Anna emerges from Josef's room, she finds the duchess, who is giving condolences to von Bohn for the fallen priest. The bishop begs pardon from the duchess to be by Anna's side.

"He'd enjoy your company," Anna tells him.

The bishop smiles and enters Josef's room. Anna and Klara are left alone. Their eyes meet.

"Annamarie?"

"He fairs well, though barely."

"That is good to hear," Klara says. "That he is doing well, I mean."

"I know what you mean."

"I am truly sorry, Annamarie."

"Good," Anna replies. "You should be."

The duchess reaches out with a consoling touch. There was a time when Anna might have accepted it, but she can see that Klara's grief for Josef is a mere tinge, as superficial as a masquerade mask. Anna pulls away. "Shouldn't you be with your husband?"

Ignoring Anna's impudence, Klara nods, then proceeds to the duke's room. There, to no surprise, she also finds Herr Weisman. Her husband's eyes are closed.

"How is he doing?" she asks.

"Resting well."

Klara *is* surprised, however, at the sight of Joop sitting on the floor in a corner of the room. "What is *that* doing here?"

"The duke has grown quite attached to it. A symbol of inspiration and hope for his future," the confidant explains. "Like the son he never had."

Klara turns from the mechanical boy to Weisman with a sneer. "Leave us. I'd like to be alone with my husband."

Herr Weisman bows and steps from the room. At the sound of the closing door—and to Klara's regret—the duke's eyes open and he takes a deep, waking breath. "Klara," he says with genuine joy.

Klara approaches the bed and takes his hand. She forces a smile. "How are you feeling, my sweet?"

"Tired but well. I was imagining I walked along a hillside, surrounded by the green of summer."

"That is a lovely thought. I expect you have many

more summers ahead of you now."

"Yes. Yes, I do now, don't I? Isn't that splendid?"

"If only the same could be said for the clockmaker."

"What do you mean?"

"He barely clings to life right now, thanks to you. Surely you considered the fact that he might not survive this. Then what?"

The duke squirms. "He has to live."

With both hands upon his great chest, Klara pushes Leopold back down and holds him there. She soothes and consoles him as though comforting a child until he settles. "That has always been the problem with you Brunners. You lack the skill for planning. You never allow for contingencies."

The duke moans. "He needs to live."

"What if he doesn't? Would that really be so horrible? You will live on. Isn't that what you want? Many more summers?"

He shakes his head. "Not like this. It's not enough."

"I'm here with you, by your side. I've been entrusted with the key to your heart, after all." She hoped her humor would bring a smile to him, but it doesn't come. She holds Leopold's head in her hands and stills it. "*Together* we will rule. Now, and for many years to come, *we* can reign."

He takes in a deep breath, then smiles faintly and closes his eyes.

"First, you must rest and heal." Klara kisses him on the cheek. "Dream of all the tomorrows you have."

The duke fades to slumber once again.

Before taking a seat across the room, the duchess reaches into her reticule and takes from it a small clock key. She examines it, folds her fingers over the benign object, then returns it to her pouch.

It is not long before Klara is lulled by the duke's sleeping drone and she, too, nods off in the uncomfortable hospital chair. It seems she has been in need of a deep rest herself. Nothing can stir her—not the constant activity of the hospital beyond the door or the visitation of nurses checking on the duke or the touch of a very small hand reaching into her reticule and removing the key. When she finally does wake, it is with a start as Herr Weisman enters.

"Pardon the intrusion, madam, but it is time to

wind your husband's heart."

Klara shakes off the remnants of slumber. "Yes. Of course. Thank you." Standing, she reaches into her pouch.

Her fingers feel around within the pouch. She removes a snuffbox. A fan. A pair of opera glasses. But no key.

Weisman asks, "Madam?"

She takes the reticule from its bottom, turns it over, and shakes it. Only a needle and thread fall to the floor. She opens the bag as wide as she can and peers inside.

"Madam? What is it?"

She searches the floor at her feet, then under the chair. She kneels awkwardly to look beneath the bed.

"You do have the key, do you not?"

"I do," Klara replies. "I *did*. I held it in my hand only moments ago." She looks at Weisman. "Is this the first you've been in here since you last left?"

Affronted by her implication, the confidant straightens his posture. "I did not sneak back in here like a common thief, if that's what you mean."

Her eyes search about the room. Her gaze stops

briefly upon Joop, who sits in the corner as motionless as the table he leans against. Shaking off a nonsensical notion, she looks one last time in her reticule. A curious smirk parts her lips. "Can the answer really have been this simple all along?"

"I'll go find someone." Weisman turns to leave.

"No."

"But if we don't do something, he'll—"

"Yes." Klara looks to her husband, firm in her decision. "We all have to die sometime."

Herr Weisman finds himself speechless.

"The duke's recovery has always been uncertain. None of us can be sure of the future. There's always been the chance that someday, his responsibilities could become my own."

"Yes, madam."

"Though I have never trusted you, Herr Weisman, your commitment to your duties is admirable. Cross me and I will have your head."

"Yes, madam." Weisman bows before exiting the room.

Klara stands in the middle of the quiet room and listens to the duke's breathing compared to her own steady, strong breaths. With a newfound clarity, she sees her place in a history to come. The duchess presses her shoulders back and calmly resumes her seat to wait.

SIXTEEN

Of

NOT DYING

There are things in this world that are beyond the scope of explanation, though poets and scientists may try: the promise of hope within a sunrise; the health benefits of hot chocolate; the emotional and spiritual power of music; a child's unconditional devotion; the perseverance of undying love; the spells of a gypsy.

Let's not forget the corruptibility of those in power, as well as their random benevolence. Klara kept the vow she made to Josef as he lay in the hospital: *I shall try to honor your example.* With her new royal authority, Duchess Brunner returned Anna's first pair of legs and the clockwork boy, Joop, to their rightful place: Kronecker's Timepieces.

The sight of the shop's front window welcomes Christoph like an old friend when he approaches one morning many months later. Inside, most of the displays have been removed, which at first concerns Christoph. Then he realizes it's a sign business has been good. He looks around at the lack of inventory until Anna appears to greet him.

"Christoph." She smiles as she makes her way across the shop's open floor. "You've been away too long. This must come as a surprise." She gestures around the shop. "We've been selling faster than Josef can create. At my insistence, he only works a few hours a day and always get a good night's sleep."

"The real surprise is that he's tolerating his new routine wholeheartedly."

"More begrudgingly than heartily, but I have my ways, you might say."

"I would say indeed." Christoph laughs and greets her with a kiss to the cheek. "How have you been, Anna?"

"Busy. Ever busy."

"Yes, of course." The doctor looks her over. "But are you well?"

"I am very well."

"Caw," interrupts Annabel, perched beside a window.

Galileo rubs himself against a table leg and then Anna's ankle, purring all the while. Christoph smiles.

"They've become quite the novelty," Anna explains. "I believe customers venture in to see them as much as they do to shop."

Their presence on the shop floor somehow feels right to Christoph, and he smiles even wider.

"You'll be staying for dinner, yes?" she asks.

"Of course. First, I must check on my patient."

"In the study."

Josef sits at his desk in a wheeled chair, with cushions stuffed behind his back for support. Drawings are spread out before him: plans for a clock of immense dimensions; sketches for another clock to fit in one's palm with straps attached; notes scrawled beside images of a new mechanism and a pair of human lungs. As usual, the clockmaker is not aware of the doctor's presence until he speaks.

"You do know the use of that chair was only meant to be temporary. You should be getting along fine without it by now."

Josef turns to his friend with a beaming grin. "I've come to find it quite comfortable, actually." He stands and they embrace—not too closely, however, because of the protrusion from Josef's chest.

Christoph acknowledges the bulge beneath the clockmaker's lounge coat. "May I?"

Josef opens his robe to reveal his new heart—its gears pumping away at a calm, steady pace—which resides outside his chest and is attached to the older device within.

"This certainly makes for an easy examination," Christoph says.

"If I've failed to mention the ingenuity of attaching the new heart to the old one, I apologize," Josef tells Christoph. "It was a brilliant idea."

"It was a matter of necessity, really. You know I didn't want to risk yet another surgery on you. Bypassing the old with the new was the only viable solution."

"Fortunately for me, our dear duke no longer needed it."

"Yes." Christoph carries on with the rest of his examination. "I will forever be puzzled as to why he didn't. It appears to be working perfectly."

"It is rather becoming, too, don't you agree?"

Josef strikes a pose, thrusting out his chest to bring his exposed, clockwork heart into full light.

Christoph laughs and glances at the papers on the desk. "What is that you're working on?"

Josef closes his coat. "A time-piece small enough to wear on your wrist. A frivolity, really."

"No. The drawing beside it. What are you concocting now?"

"That is a mechanized lung, to assist anyone who might suffer with labored breathing."

Christoph leans in for a closer look, then gives a long, skeptical groan.

For dinner, the three friends enjoy a meal of roasted lamb and potatoes prepared by Gretchen, the flower girl, who Anna recently hired. Afterward, they talk of common things, like torte and the coming summer. Anna shares news of shops opening around the city; Christoph tells of his return to Vienna and his new position with the university.

"While teaching offers its own challenges," he says, "the daily pressure is much less than running a practice."

"You don't miss seeing patients?" Anna asks.

"I still conduct an occasional examination and consult with other physicians. But, no, I'm enjoying simpler days of late. My life has taken a welcomed turn."

Josef gives him an approving, peaceful grin. "The hand of an idyllic life touches ever so gently, doesn't it? Almost imperceptibly. If I've learned anything, it is to never look away for it may be missed. No one knows what lies ahead nor can we control it. All one can truly see is the moment."

"Spoken like a poet." Christoph nods, then grins. "Another pleasant development."

"Speaking of poetry, have you experienced Pascal's most recent concerto?"

"I attended a performance of his in Venice a few weeks back. How he conducted the orchestra with his handless left arm while he played with his right was remarkable. I would venture to say the artistry of his compositions have reached unparalleled sublimity—introspective and deeply morose one moment and life-affirming the next."

Anna drops her gaze. "A broken heart will do that."

Josef puts a hand on her wrist. "That's how

broken hearts mend."

She looks back with reticent comfort.

"That's why I hung up that painting from behind my worktable," Josef adds with a reassuring squeeze to her hand.

Christoph gives a quizzical look. "Painting?"

Anna grins. "Josef may be of exemplary intellect in many ways, but in others he is like any ordinary man, easily swayed by a woman's charm and beauty. He never saw that those of the duchess went only as deep as her flesh."

Josef huffs. "I did eventually."

Anna laughs and continues her explanation for Christoph. "Her ruse was so calculated that even I thought Klara had beguiled him with the gift of a painting—a portrait of her in her younger days. I found it while cleaning one day and considered throwing it out."

"It turns out it wasn't a portrait of Klara," Josef says.

Curiosity furrows Christoph's forehead, then his eyes open wide. "May I see it?"

The three of them make their way to Josef's

study. There, hanging on the wall opposite Josef's desk, is a portrait Christoph did not notice before, of a woman aglow with the optimism of youth, her features not yet aged to exquisite maturity. Christoph sighs at the captivating image. "Your wife, Isabelle. The likeness is…"

Josef nods. "Remember I said there was something strangely familiar about the duchess? Uncanny, is it not?"

"I myself hadn't considered the resemblance—until now, that is."

Josef indicates the lower part of the painting. "If you look closely."

"She is with child. Oh, I remember when she sat for this. She was so happy that day."

"It's easy to see that distractions got the better of me." The clockmaker directs an apologetic gaze to his assistant. "It's almost forgivable."

Anna leans in to give him a gentle kiss on the cheek. "Only just."

🕐 ❧ 🕐 ❧ 🕐

The sun warms Anna's face. Together with Galileo's

purring from the foot of the bed, it draws her from sleep. She rises with the decision not to wear her right hand this day. She does this on occasion just to know she can. If her ex-lover Pascal can compose and conduct one-handed concertos, she can manage her mundane chores one-handed once in a while. Of course, she'll continue to walk on her Josef-given legs. It would be absurd not to.

Anna spends the morning in the comfort of routine. It is an important ingredient of the aforementioned idyllic life. The never-ending winding of clocks, dusting, and tending to the menagerie—she cherishes it all. Noticing the box of Joop's discs out on a worktable, she lifts and places it on an upper shelf.

Her favorite part of the morning is spent playing a game.

She knows he's there, usually hiding behind one of the bin-filled shelves or stalking her from behind a stack of boxes. Her heart warms at the sound of feet shuffling from one shadowed nook to another. Anna swears she hears him giggle, though she knows that's not possible. She doesn't turn around when he finally emerges, but instead allows him to sneak up on her and waits for him to grab the hem of her apron or her hand. Letting out a squeal that startles the rats, Anna turns with playful, exaggerated shock. The little boy's mouth opens in voiceless delight, and his moonstone eyes sparkle with life. On Anna's face is the glow of a mother's love.

"Joop! What have I said about scaring people?"

Author Note

Every writer aspires (or *should* aspire)
for an all-important author-editor partnership.
I've become fortunate enough to have two.
First, Andrea Beatrice Reed
(AndreaBeatriceReed@yahoo.com) turned my
manuscript upside-down and inside-out
developmentally, vastly improving it in too
many ways to list here.
Then, through Blue Pen Books, I connected with
Chelsea Cambeis (chelseacambeis.com), whose
Line Editing polished my book into what
I think is my best so far.
Thank you both.
I look forward to working with you again.

Gordon Gravley has called the Northwest United States his home for over two decades now. There, he writes and publishes, hoping to someday produce a book people will actually want to read. *Of Gilded Flesh* is his third novel. You can subscribe to his monthly newsletter *Chasing Words* via his website.

GENRE
GAMUT
BOOKS